CRUSHING DREAMS

A Benny Wright Story: Book 1
Based on the Award-Winning Musical,
Wrapped

Dennis A Nehamen

Golden Poppy Publications
Los Angeles

Crushing Dreams
By Dennis A Nehamen

Copyright © 2017 Dennis A Nehamen
All Rights Reserved

Published by Golden Poppy Publications™
Los Angeles, CA
www.dennisnehamen.com

ISBN: 978-1-945329-14-2

Library of Congress Control Number: 2016939740

Lyrical Passages by Craig M Nehamen

Cover by Cline Cover Design

Nehamen, Dennis A Author

Crushing Dreams

Dennis A Nehamen

Printed in the United States of America

First Edition

Benny Wright was inspired from an archetype of the human male. Jewel Wright, his wife, likewise, I perceived as the quintessence of the counterpart human female. Together it was my intent to portray them as representative of the most profound love that can be realized from a marital union. Then destiny played a wild card, and "one" simple circumstance wreaked havoc on the joy they shared together as man and woman—a word to the wise about cheating in romantic relationships.

I dedicate this book to my wife, Bernice. Never have I had a day of misery wondering about her faithfulness to our bond. I owe what little success that I credit myself with in great part to this fact.

PROLOGUE

"Cut!" shouted the interviewer, as he aggressively stretched his hand to back off the dollied camera moving in for a close-up shot.

"Mr. Wright, let's try it one more time...but...without the tears."

"I don't think I can do that."

"We just don't want to portray you as less than the man you are."

"I'm Benny Wright. You'll have to take me as I am," I responded with less irascibility than humility.

"It has nothing to do with how I take you. It's for...the people who are going to see this."

"Why don't you ask me another question?" I suggested.

"Fine," the man acquiesced. "Let's take it again, Morry," he snapped to his producer. "Now, Mr. Wright, you mentioned in your notes that during your journey you discovered the conditions under which Gods are born."

"That's right, Mr. Conrad, I did. My friend alluded to it but I filled in the blanks."

"I'm certain there are many people out there who would like to hear about that," he chuckled. "Well, when is it that this miracle occurs?"

"It's very simple actually. When man stands alone, crying…terrified…friendless…that's when we create our deities."

"Let's get back to your music," Conrad swiftly turned to a new subject. "The material you wrote for *Wrapped*… what was the inspiration for the majestic sounds and lyrics we're hearing?"

"I thought you didn't want me to cry."

CHAPTER 1: I CLOSE MY EYES

It must have happened at the moment I was born, for I recall no specific moment in my early life when a judicial decree was issued, ordering me, Benny Wright, to write music and lyrics, and then perform my work. Looking back, I always approached what I'll call my life pursuit with thrill and enthusiasm. I never conceived that what sparked my creative passion could turn into a punishment; at least not until I reached my mid-thirties, when a crushing event took place that moved my center of gravity from safe planet earth to a mercurial, mischievous, and mocking star in a remote galaxy.

Throughout the experience I bucked and kicked, throwing a tantrum that would inflict unimaginable and unprecedented suffering on the people I loved most.

It was April 14, 2012, a Sunday morning, when the adventure I'm about to relate began. I remember it precisely. I was lying in bed with my wife, Jewel. It was a gorgeous spring sunrise. I loved to sleep with the shutters open. The rays filtered through the leaves of the two giant white ash trees that sheltered our house.

I'd concealed for over a week a secret that was itching to be betrayed. I felt like a little boy with a nagging urge to be naughty. Neither Jewel nor the children knew that I was flying to New York the next morning. My wish was to surprise them when I returned with the good news of my first real contract. I intended to drop the New York deal on the table and then watch as they celebrated.

So, while we talked about our plans for the day, I told Jewel that I had agreed to a double shift to help out a friend. I let her know I'd be leaving that evening for work and not returning until late the next afternoon. It wasn't out of the ordinary, so she thought nothing of it. We stayed in bed until about eight, when the children woke up.

Jewel was in the kitchen, making us some pancakes and bacon, and I was in the living room doing what I loved most—making music, whipping up fantasy and singing one of my tunes. As the magic swirled, I thought of the way our family was ordered. Jewel was the steel and wood beams, the bones comprising the skeletal structure, as well as the muscle systems steadying its sway and movement. It was her steadfastness that allowed the rest of us to swing freely, knowing we were safe and secure on the end of a tether.

That morning, I invited the children into the dream image I was enacting. I had created the piece, and both my sprouting teenage son Dion and his younger sister Shana were written in. They each already knew their parts. It was pretty cool—the three actors on our own imaginary stage, swinging to the beat of a sweet hip-hop musical performance while momma bear flipped hotcakes in the kitchen.

"What do you see, son?" I sang out to my boy, Dion, as he shimmied to the center of the living room.

"I see my fans in one hand and a mic in the other, Pop."

With unrestrained excitement, Shana vaulted into the room and stood next to her brother. "I see myself on a stage of dancers, front and center."

"I see those fans and that mic. I see that stage of dancers," I exclaimed, my eyes ever so subtly beginning to close.

"That's all you see, Pop? Only what Dion and I see? That's all you see when you close your eyes?" Shana posed as she intentionally led me deeper into my role.

"Oh, Shana…"

I'd recorded the music for "I Close My Eyes" and had it ready to go. I hit the *Play* button and the sound filled the house. My stage name was *Magic*. I had positioned myself just outside the room where the children now stood, and from there, like an announcer, I called out "Magic" over the din of music. I had lifted my right arm, with my index finger extended toward the sky. Then, I suddenly dropped the gesture and ran to join my children, like I was the main act coming on stage at the Madison Square Garden.

The piece was all about the dreams in my mind's eye and how the world comes alive in the inner space of my imagination. It was about the wonder of being alive.

"All I gotta do is just close my eyes and everything inside me comes alive. All I gotta do is just close my eyes, hopin' one day I'll open them and see it's my life.

I winked at the children. Their faces glistened, awaiting me to continue a routine they'd rehearsed many times with me.

"I close my eyes and the stage is mine, twenty thousand people and lights that blind. I close my eyes and people stand aligned, beggin' for a piece of my time. I close my eyes and I'm a fountain of fame, the topic of talk shows, new to the game. I close my eyes and my children live in vain, and complain during trips to Spain."

"Daddy, this is my favorite verse," Shana yelled to me, urging me to continue my performance.

I replied with a thumbs-up. It was some of my best writing.

"I close my eyes and I awaken on cue, to watch as my family travels by cruise. An ocean of sky and a sky of music, I'm lost in a daze of awe and amusement."

"I got it, Pop," Dion sang out, announcing that his lines were next up.

"I close my eyes and I'm rapped in rap songs, basked

10

in claps in a crowd of passion. A mass of fans that dance while I grasp them, cheer when I ask and boo when I'm absent."

"Daddy! Daddy!" Shana exclaimed so nobody could mistake it was her turn.

"I close my eyes and I wake up quick, to laughin' on a family trip. Foolish swimmin' in a swimming pool, and days upon days with no school."

We sang and sang, over and over about all we wished for our futures, individually and together. It was so real, as if we just had to close our eyes, fantasize, and in a matter of time, the fruits of our dream world would be the feasts of our lives.

While the children were performing the chorus, I ran into the kitchen to get Jewel. "Well, hello gorgeous," I smiled as I dragged her to join us. She stood and watched. After we finished, I addressed her again. "Jewel, we were just in the process of closing our eyes...and I was seein' you like a princess in a shrine, my bright jewel." She sparkled like a gem.

Jewel was beautiful. She could have been a stand-in for Beyonce Knowles if the star were ill, the only giveaway being the creamy-yellowish hue to her skin that was shades lighter. Determining her cultural background was more challenging than bringing peace to the Middle East. She'd joke that she might represent every country in the United Nations. Off the top of her head she could account for white, American Indian,

European Spanish, along with French, Creole, and Jewish blood.

Needless to say, race never played much of a role in our lives. In fact, my light skin tone, due to my African-American father and my Caucasian mom, might have left a curious observer giving up on how to classify me.

I recall standing in front of Jewel that morning with my eyes pressed closed for some time before I opened them. I walked over to the player and pressed *Stop.* It was a joyous occasion. We were all together, and it was the best of the best of experiences multiplied by infinity.

I looked over at Shana and laughed. She's a kid forever in perpetual motion, a real ham. When we broke from the song, Jewel called out for Shana to help with setting the table. As if the rhythm of the song were still alive in her soul, propelling her to move, she skipped into the kitchen.

The conversations that morning are recorded in my permanent memory. Jewel stared at our daughter with a look that was a mixture of love and astonishment.

"What is in your veins, girl?"

"Don't know."

"Well, whatever it is…slow…it…down," Jewel advised, intentionally drawing out her words to emphasize the reduced pace she hoped to elicit from Shana.

"No…slow…gear," was Shana's answer.

I was gagging as I watched the exchange. Shana,

making her best attempt to please her mom, practically stopped to hit each letter, but her little body was still gyrating like a spinning top as she danced around the table, dropping knives and forks like notes in her own composition.

Dion couldn't resist joining in the banter. "She jitters while she sleeps, Mom."

"If you were dreamin' what I'm dreamin', you'd be jittering too."

To make her point, Shana spontaneously performed a full cartwheel across the room.

"I think you're missing the whole point of sleep, Shana."

Her big brother intended to enlighten the sapling but he should have known better. He'd made the same mistake repeatedly in the past—we all did. Shana was not only an energetic child but a precocious one as well. My daughter could extemporaneously talk on subjects most children her age might not have even considered, and do so with a lyrically inventive spirit that would at times leave her audience wondering if she were reciting poetry. Her next speech was an example.

"You know sleeping is a waste of time. Most people are just fine without a third of their life in recline. If every person were to sleep a bit less, say about half that, there'd be..." She slowed to calculate. "20 billion hours of energy excess—per day! That's enough to launch a rocket to Pluto, enough to produce two hundred fifty thousand new cars or..."

"*You* have enough energy to produce a hundred thousand..."

"Claps, cheers, and roars?" She rapidly paced her retort, dulling her brother's jibe.

Even Dion had to adore her in the end. There was something about Shana that could be phenomenally annoying, yet draw you in. At those times, you couldn't get enough of her. That morning, her brother made no attempt to continue the dialogue. The aroma of the sizzling bacon and the vision of hotcakes on the table compelled him to drop her like a bad draw at a poker table.

The rest of the day was awesome. It was one of those dreamy memories that you can easily bring to awareness, but after doing so, you can't decide if it would be best to dissolve it in acid or embrace it and never let it go. How can a world so wonderful one instant, be so quickly transformed into hell—without you having even a vague idea what you did or didn't do to cause it?

I left the house close to eleven thirty that evening. From the car, I called the HR office to notify them I wouldn't be coming in for the morning shift, which was actually all I was scheduled to handle the next day. Ecstatic, I drove to the airport. The flight was not that long, so I had hours to burn on both ends of the trip. I didn't need to be at their office until nine in the morning.

The flight was uneventful, with the exception of one

minor hiccup. I had the window seat, and a young couple occupied the center and aisle. The problem was they were each holding infants, identical twin girls only two months old. These newborns didn't know night from day and performed a discordant duet throughout the entire flight. I had planned to catch a couple hours sleep but was never permitted a wink.

It didn't matter much. I was so jacked up on the thrill I could have forfeited rest for a week and never known the difference. Ever since I was a boy younger than Dion, I was possessed by a drive to create music. I'd sneak out of the house late at night, when my parents thought I was sleeping, to stand outside some of the local clubs and listen to the players. I participated in every band, orchestra, and theater production in school. I formed a jazz quartet of my own by the time I was twelve. I knew in my heart that I was destined to write and perform my own material.

I carried on with the dream right up to and through my marriage and the starting of our family. Sure, I was so convincing about my prospect for fame that I hooked Jewel into my fantasy, and later the children. But, I made them pay. I persisted in devoting myself to my craft, and later had to admit that I had cheated them, that had I buckled down on my career I would have succeeded monetarily and provided better for them... yet they still stood by me. It was one close call after another, as I breathed hope into the fame-will-be-right-around-the-corner dream, each time leading to greater disappointment.

If I'm going to be forthright, then I have to fess up to the reality that there is a point where you just can't believe in yourself any longer. A person can take only so many messages of rejection. I'd submitted songs that I'd written at least a hundred times and been promised that artists were going to produce them. Several times, there were record labels ready to sign me to recording deals, but for one reason or another, those contracts always fell through. I'd perform live at clubs and be told by recording executives that I was a guaranteed star, but they'd never follow up by calling me afterward.

After years of hoping and yearning, it can get very dangerous to think about continuing. How many times can you fail, be so close, slammed to the mat and whipped, and then still come back for more? Can it get so bad that you're willing to risk everything—your wife, your children and all the things in your life you proclaim to love? Bad enough that you're groveling like a gambler, stealing quarters from your children's lunch money to place another wager; or stinking from the smoke of a filthy bar you can't resist visiting for just one more shot of cheap rum? It's a terrible addiction.

I did work regularly to provide for them. But what was the reward for my toil? A few bucks from a lousy auto factory job to keep poverty and hopelessness dangling in front of us like rotting carrots on a stick. I'm not a dumb, uneducated guy either. I did well in school, all the way to college, up to completing a four-year degree. In fact, what motivated me most about school was music. To me, the composition of a song and the lyrics were about language and mathematics. I majored in both because I believed they would elevate the standard of my art.

Then, in order to be able to pursue my career as an entertainer, I took the job at the factory, doing similar work to what my father had done to support his family. I love my dad. I respect him for the sacrifices that he made for all of us. But I wanted more. I knew that many of my fellow students from high school and college found their way to success as professionals, leaders, and businesspeople. I was certain I would find my reward through my creative talents. It was a promise that I had made to my family. I told them that I'd provide for them several levels higher than what my dad had been able to accomplish. So far, I'd not kept my pledge.

Things were about to change. Yes, New York, here I come! At last, after riding the fast-jerking, up-and-down thrusting of the music biz pogo stick, I was on my way to signing my first big contract—my agent had negotiated an album, a concert tour, and a guaranteed promotional budget. It wasn't enormous, but it was far more than the near nothing I'd achieved up to this point and enough for me to leave home gloating that I had a handful of four-leaf clovers. My problems were about to end. I was finally going to give my family everything I had all but guaranteed them. The pain of doubt and the seduction of hope were over. Benny Wright had arrived.

When I departed for The Big Apple, my thoughts were not in New York. I was already back home, gleaming as I watched Jewel read the fine print of a record deal that would assure our next step—a move to one flank of the country or the other, either to Los Angeles or New York. By the following evening, together with my love, I'd be planning to "watch as my family travels by cruise, an ocean of sky and a sky of music." Benny Wright and his clan "lost in a daze of awe and amusement."

CHAPTER 2: LET'S WRAP THIS BABY UP

I wandered around New York City for a several hours before the meeting. I recall eating a bagel and lox for breakfast at Carnegie's Deli at the corner of 7th Avenue and 55th Street before the sun peeked out. With so much time to kill, I thought of shopping for gifts for the family, but most of the retail stores were still closed.

Then in no time, the main streets were packed with cars and humans. I wondered how so many people could be in such a hurry at the same time. How many important matters could be taking place at the same exact instant? The mass of humanity looked like the chaotic frenzy of bees swarming around a hive. But as I stopped in one spot and watched, I realized that each separate unit of mankind was purposeful in a singular pursuit that served the whole no different than worker bees blindly functioning in the service of the queen.

New York City was their hive, the sacred queen shrouded somewhere in the bowels of the concrete, earth, and steel matter. But who was the king, I wondered. Who impregnated the queen so that she could give birth to her army of faithful soldiers? I would soon have my answer.

I moseyed along the busy avenues and occasionally detoured laterally along some of the less populated side streets. It was there that I came upon some vagrants who were still sleeping. Some of the more prosperous ones were honored to rest in dirty sleeping bags discarded by more affluent residents. But there were also many lying motionless in their street clothing—I was repulsed by the stench and appearance of urine and feces-stained fabrics dampened by cheap spirits.

At first, it seemed no different than what I frequently observed in parts of Detroit. But then it dawned on me that it was not the same—at home I rarely paid attention to them. They seemed now, as I strolled along the pavement, human beings with histories no different than the wealthy and successful residents of the neighborhood where they took refuge, cuddled next to the stoops of buildings or alongside trash containers.

I tried to calculate how many unexpected events had to happen to a little child before they ended up living dismally on the streets, with no hope of ever reclaiming their duty in the service of one queen or another. My circumstance placed me at a distance from these sad souls, but I was not oblivious to how much suffering I had endured nor to the thought that it might be possible the people I was now feeling charity toward had only taken one more blow than I to land at the end of the line.

Then it hit me, a frightful conclusion. Precisely how many bad breaks did it take before a person lost their will to try? The question suggested that there was a finite number and it differed for each of the fractured beings I passed like broken toys or wilted flowers. But the answer to my question of how many blows it takes to rupture the soul was absurdly simple. It was one, one single event.

Every person on the street—in my hometown of Detroit, or in New York, San Francisco, Paris, Budapest, or Moscow—any individual in any tiny community around the globe, had given their all to be part of the productive endeavor of building hives. At some point, however, an experience of enormous proportion, or even minimal measurement, sacked their will. Sure, everything that proceeded was a contribution, everybody took their bruises in life, but for these people on the street it was that *one* thing that did them in.

I recall shivering, a frightful sensation, as one inkling of reality seeped in, one idea that I refused to permit to lease a space in my consciousness—the thought of my own oneness with these lost souls. At some moment in his life, could Benny Wright face that single event, the "one" critical circumstance that would sap his lust for dreaming of something better? I never went so far as to chip away at the question, but I remember standing and quivering for some time before I looked at my watch and realized it was nearly time for me to meet the destiny I had been called to New York to fulfill.

I was only a few blocks from my destination, Avenue of the Stars, between 47th and 48th Streets. When I arrived and stared up at the colossal in front of me, I read the sign RAVISH RECORDS over the main entrance. My heart stalled as I imagined the glory the future now held for my family and me.

It reinforced the awareness that for the first time, I had truly arrived as an artist. I'm a kid born and raised in Delray. It is an unimpressive Detroit neighborhood. Yet, all two yards of my height stood taller than a giant in front of a sixty-seven-story building owned by my new record label, a structure proudly elevated high enough to speak fraternally to the gods above. I walked into the lobby and rode that elevator to the sixty-sixth floor. I might have owned the place.

The first sign of trouble occurred when I went into the reception area and the secretary searched the appointment books of Mr. Caruso and Ms. Toleen—to see if Benny Wright had been scheduled. It had been penciled in and subsequently erased.

"There has to be a mistake, miss. They arranged for

me to fly in for a meeting this morning," I casually informed her.

"I'm sorry, Mr. Wright, but there's nothing I can do."

"No, you don't understand. Mr. Caruso…"

"Sir, I know all that but I can assure you the meeting has been cancelled."

I frantically took out my cell phone. I was about to call my manager when, by chance, I spotted Caruso and Toleen walking together through the interior hallway just behind the reception desk.

"Mr. Caruso," I cried out loud enough to capture the attention of the whole office. He glanced my way. When he looked at me, his mouth widened with the grandest of smiles. His teeth were huge; the sight of them made me freeze in terror as I imagined these sword-sharp weapons were about to impale me.

He hesitated. I don't believe he recalled my name, but I noticed that Toleen whispered in her associate's ear.

"Magic! We'll be in touch," Caruso finally waved, magnanimously gesturing his acknowledgement that I had once existed as a distant speck in his universe.

"Hold on," I demanded. "I'm here to sign the deal. You had me flown in."

Caruso was a large, fashionably dressed, handsome man. He walked over to where I stood on the opposite side of the waiting area and greeted me warmly.

"Didn't you get the message? We emailed you this morning."

"I flew in before you woke up," I informed him with notable irritation.

"Well, don't take it personally. Our A&R Director did a last-minute review of your latest tracks and had second doubts about how your image would work for our lineup. We had to nix the deal," he explained with a matter-of-fact expression that felt assaultive. "Don't worry. We'll be keeping you in mind."

"Please, Mr. Caruso, I was told all I had to do was sign and meet some of the people I'd be working with. My agent, Garland, said every detail of the contract had been agreed upon."

Caruso patted me on the shoulder, a pitiful token of comfort for a man witnessing himself mortally wounded. "It's a wild business. Don't give up," he said as he raced back to the inner office, Toleen speed-walking to keep abreast of her partner.

I stood with my eyes closed. I had no lyrics left, but I did have an answer to the question of who was king of the beehive—Brandon Caruso.

I went downstairs and found a bench. I had dressed in a loose-fitting, collarless white linen shirt with black baggy slacks. As I sat alone, I repeatedly tilted my head sideways and let the collar of my shirt sop up the tears streaming down my cheeks like clear blood. My heart had been ripped from me, and I behaved as a man would after finding himself heartless—absent of all feeling, numb and disoriented.

It may have been a synopsis born of bitterness, but for the first time I thought I understood the essence of the music business as never before. I had no doubt that Brandon Caruso was the king. He was the impregnator of the queen, the ruler of something greater than the hive he left to his darling like a large diamond rock she could wear on her finger, each facet magically beaming to create an endless series of workers to serve her purpose. In this arena of nature, however, the king was no victim of his lover. He didn't perish after knocking up his sweetheart, but instead, dominated her and everything else in his kingdom.

What was his domain? Music. Men like Brandon Caruso owned the sole unifying principle of mankind. He understood that humans were motivated by fear, a primary drive that manifested itself in hatred, violence, betrayal, dishonor, slander, and every other indecent behavior of man. Humans unconscionably killed neighbors they worried might be plotting to steal their land or lover; waged wars against their own people, due to a difference in allegiance to God; and attempted to annihilate whole races of people due to their skin color, beliefs or traditions—all governed by fright.

Caruso also recognized that from the most diverse backgrounds on the planet, humans could be brought together and then delivered to a state of transcendence from terror by the infinite variations of sound—the pulse, rhythm, melody, cadence, and beat of music.

25

Most importantly, the masses of people could be enfeebled by the sounds they were subjected to as well as the messages contained in the lyrics.

The essential elements of music could be used more effectively than explosive weapons to indoctrinate people to a way of thinking and feeling—their behaviors and thoughts easily brought under the domination of the music they listened to, their minds controlled so they could be subjugated by power mongers like Caruso. Brandon Caruso knew it—he was king. He determined who would be permitted to sing to the troops in the trenches, as well as which messages they would deliver.

I had been stepped on like the bug I should have known myself to be. My membership card to a club of distinguished servants permitted to perform on Caruso's stage had been torn up in front of my face even before my name was ink-dried on the paper. My eyes remained closed as I conjured these thoughts. I was consumed with wonderment. How could I have been such a fool as to believe that Benny Wright, a nothing from Delray, Detroit, Michigan, might have earned admission to such an esteemed world?

"No! No! No!" The words jeered as they paraded in my conscious mind. All the glory I had dreamed would be mine was a mirage. It would never happen. Benny Wright had just died.

Whether I was partially or totally—or not at all— correct in my assessment of music as a political tool, it was of little consequence to the anguish of my life at that moment. I couldn't lift myself off the bench. All I wanted to do was cuddle up with the slugs on the street. There I could await death without the agony of another sunrise, another pearly executive's false smile, another mortifying moment of shame, knowing that I was leading my family on a perilous journey destined to end at the worst threshold of possibility—in mediocrity.

It was a nasty upbraiding, the beginning of a series of tyrannical beatings my ego was about to take. The energy of my sense of despair wouldn't be exhausted until, like a black hole, it had sucked in and fully swallowed not only the guilt I shamed on myself, but also my innocence.

After a period of time, the raging and pitiless feelings drifted away, replaced by what I can best describe as a sense of emotional nothingness, a state of nonexistence. I have no idea how I made it to the airport or any recall of the flight back to Detroit. I surmise that some sort of robotic execution of actions with no conscious deliberation or drive dictated the necessary steps for me to reach home.

Back in Detroit, I might have designated myself a tragic hero, but such a kind term was undeserved. The date I flew back from New York was April 15th. It had not been a good day, and the evening was going to be crowned with a mortal nightcap—a bad day, bad night.

CHAPTER 3: BLOODY BAD LUCK

My car was parked at the airport. After I picked it up, I must have decided to stop off for a beer. In my despaired state, the last thing I wanted to do was to go back to the house. Normally, I'd have visited *Jimbo's*, a tiny spot near our home, where I'd horse around with the guys. I'm guessing, but probably the reason I did the unexpected was that I couldn't bear the thought of seeing anybody familiar. That evening I drove my car and left it around the block from Wally's Liquor on Bagley Street.

I never made it into the store, I'm sure of that. I wandered aimlessly from one street to another, seeking an ointment to heal my wounded soul. Suddenly, out of the quiet of the night, I heard rapid steps. Someone was racing frantically on the concrete sidewalk. Then I heard a male voice scream a terrifying noise, an adolescent-sounding outburst that jolted me from my mental cocoon.

As I began to process what was happening, I understood why the fellow was panicked. Within an instant, a vehicle made a screeching sound and rounded the corner where the man had just turned. The car accelerated. As it closed in on the figure dashing full-speed down the street, I noticed two stick-like objects projecting out from the passenger side of the car.

It was a Jeep with no license plates. The car slowed as it came up alongside the man and paused long enough for the rifles to open fire. The sound was like a hundred shots blasting through the stillness of the evening air. I saw the machine-gunned man go down to the ground. A heavy mist enveloped the scene, making it impossible to see who had done the shooting or to make out the identity of the victim. The driver gunned the engine, and the Jeep's wheels skidded on the slick pavement. As the unidentifiable car attempted its getaway, the backside of the vehicle jumped the curb, coming within a few feet of hitting me.

Noticing my presence, the driver slammed on the brakes. I was sure they were going to gun me down too. I saw vague faces in the vehicle. I knew that I'd never be able to identify any of them. I prayed they had realized that too. Fortunately, the man behind the wheel accelerated a second time. He drove to the end of the block and stopped, leaving the engine idling. It was my opportunity to take off running in the opposite direction, yet I couldn't. I have no idea why I felt compelled to do so—but I needed to try and help the slain man. I took a deep breath and turned back toward the victim, grateful that his assailants hadn't tried to kill me. At least for the moment, my life had been spared.

I was, at most, fifty feet from where the man lay bleeding. However, even from that distance, I still couldn't make out who he was. Surprisingly, not one person had come out of their home to investigate. I realized I was alone at the scene of a crime—except for the shooters in the Jeep who remained at the corner for a few more seconds before taking off.

Instinctively, I ran to the man to see if I could help. That's when I saw that he was no more than eighteen years old. The kid had taken an unimaginable number of bullets, the most gruesome to the throat, which made him appear like a fountain that had tumbled over; he was pumping red like a broken faucet. He grabbed at his right shoulder that had been nearly severed by the explosion of shell casings.

He seemed to be entreating me to come nearer. Honestly, after getting closer, I wanted to run. I had never seen a human being shot. The scene was so ghastly that I could hardly tolerate looking. Finally, I did put my head down toward him. To my amazement, and disgust, he took his blood-dripping hand and reached it around my neck to pull me still closer. That's when I could see that the blood loss had turned his facial skin from white to a deathly looking dull yellow color. He whispered his last words in my ear—it was like a scene from a movie I hope to never see again.

"Sometimes we have to do the right thing, even if we die…"

I watched the young fellow expire. I couldn't say for certain if he had more to say after the word "die" or if he had finished his sentence with that word.

Somebody must have looked out their window and called the police, because the next thing I recall was the siren blast of another vehicle heading toward where I sat in a state of shock on the ground next to the dead victim. Because it seemed as if hardly any time had passed, I was certain the same men were coming back to finish off the sole witness to the shooting.

Of course, they never would have had a siren, but my mind was not processing things correctly. As the car approached, I couldn't tell that it was a police vehicle, a fact that made me even more certain my time had come. I held my breath, awaiting my end. Before exhaling, I realized that it was an unmarked detective car.

The sole officer jumped out and ran over to me. He flashed a badge and identified himself as Detective Bix Rafferty. Within seconds, the sound of other vehicles filled the air. Rafferty asked me a few questions and then left me sitting on the curb for several minutes while he talked with what seemed like a battalion of law enforcement officials who had converged on the scene. Then he came back to me.

"I want to make sure. Did you know the man?" Rafferty repeated a question he'd definitely asked earlier.

"No, sir. As I told you, I happened by chance to be out here walking."

"What about the driver? You're sure you couldn't make out details of the car or driver?"

"I'm positive. Look, I had a bad day. I don't know a thing. I really don't recall any specifics."

"Do you have some identification?"

I reached for my wallet and handed Rafferty my driver's license, watching as he wrote down the information. By now, several residents were observing the scene from a distance, and it was only a minute later when I heard the siren of what I knew was an ambulance that would be serving as a hearse on this occasion.

"What about a phone number?" Rafferty asked.

"(313) 760-2349," I answered.

"Look, if you want to go, we can get in touch with you later should we need you."

He must have noticed I looked dazed because he made a kind offer.

"I'll have one of the boys take you home in a few minutes."

"It's okay. Thanks."

I had no idea that my face, neck, and upper coat were wet from fresh blood. Jewel did the instant I came in the front door. She let out a shout. Then she ran to me and wrapped her arms around my body. I noticed she squeezed with all her power. I also recognized that my physical self was as unresponsive as the dead man I'd just left.

For a husband Jewel knew to be affectionate, the first sign of danger noted by my wife had to be when she recognized that I offered no reaction. Of course, she tried to elicit from me what had happened, and I managed to explain about my chance witnessing of a young man being gunned down—but I never said a word about New York.

Spiritless, I showered, had dinner, and went to sleep early. The next day, I put in a full shift. Upon my arrival home that afternoon, I said nothing to Jewel other than perfunctory comments about work and the children—she read me like a clock. My wife was right to be alarmed, although she didn't understand the extent of it. I had been doubly traumatized—New York and then the murder. I was about to set Jewel, our children, and me on a Disneyesque wild, wild ride. Benny Wright was a shameful failure; there was going to be no tonic to soothe that bitter reality.

"Sometimes we have to do the right thing, even if we die…"

Those were the last words of a dying man, and he'd shared them with me. They had no significance as far as I could tell, yet I couldn't stop repeating them, syllable by syllable. I had no idea why. I also had no way of knowing that I was about to engage in a series of bumbling experiments, flirting with fate, taking chance to the outer limits where dreams are bought and sold like worthless scam parcels of property in remote deserts.

While Jewel was calculating how much time she needed to allow me to come to her and share my hurt, her wounded husband was diving deeper into despair. My full focus had come back to the breaking of the contract by Caruso and his people at Ravish Records. They had shattered my hopes and plans for my family by twisting the first several inches of a long steel screw mortally through my heart. It only took *one*, the last in a series of impalements surgically aimed into my soul with the effect of bleeding out my zest for living.

The day after I came home, I placed a call to my agent and manager, Garland. I have to confess holding on to a smidgen of hope that it was either a big joke or a misunderstanding. *Could the deal still be breathing?* I asked myself in a desperate attempt to find the sunny side of the street in a whiteout. When he didn't call me back, however, the matter was resolved. By then, in truth, I knew it was over. I had finally reconciled myself to the fact that my days of pursuing music as a career were finished. The problem was that I hadn't begun to address how I would atone for having deprived Jewel and the children through my selfish wish for fame.

Garland and I go back to grade school. He's a very

successful and powerful man in the industry. He measures over six-feet-six. He was a star basketball and football player in high school, doted over by most of the popular girls. Garland was fairly bright in academics, possessed a remarkably swelled ego, and was sought after by most of the coolest guys in the class. He was also outgoing, friendly, humorous, lighthearted, and…a bull-shitter of such extraordinary achievement, he'd have made a perfect candidate for public office.

Everyone tolerated his warped and deficient character because he always had gifts to dispense that people were eager to attain—unfortunately, far less of them were ever delivered than promised. Still, he was a relic from "back in the day" who I had hoped would be the catalyst to my career launch.

Garland had a way about him. When he arrived at a given space and time, it was like an invasion. His personality was highly dynamic and infectious. As a result, there was always a fan base dreaming they might share in the wonder of his presence.

We had just finished dinner the evening after the disastrous day of my trip to New York and the murder. The family was in what I ironically called the "grand room" of our home. Our dwelling was modest at best, but this space was by far the largest. I believe anyone entering our home would have immediately recognized it as the heart of the house, the inner chamber, the pulsing, breathing organ that fed the vital life substance through the family members' veins and arteries so that we could thrive as individuals and as a unit.

Dion's instruments, including a guitar and keyboard, were housed in one corner, facing an easterly wall. To his right, was a large window that looked out toward the neighbor's yard. On the other side of the window, across the room, Shana had a desk where she did her home-work—our children each had their own bedrooms. They were so small, however, that there was barely space for their beds and dressers.

The sofa faced the front yard, deep at the rear of the room, and adjacent, there were two matching comfort-able chairs. The only television in our home was sitting on a stand that faced the couch. TV was not a big item for any of us, although we each had a favorite show that we routinely tuned into. The master of the palace was rewarded his own office, a closet-sized enclosure where I kept my instruments and recording equipment. There I sat, staring blankly into space. When the doorbell rang, Shana ran to get it. Unannounced, Garland showed up.

"What's up, buddy?" he called out to me as if he had just returned from a winning Tigers' game. As he waltzed through the room, he flattered each of the family members. "Hello, hello. Dion, future client, VIP; Sha-na, the hottest thing in junior high; and, Jewel, the hot-test thing…since junior high. Benny, my greatest friend."

"Garland, oh distinguished one, what brings you

here?" I listlessly responded on behalf of the whole family.

"Benny, buddy, we have to talk."

He took me by the arm and led me toward the dining room where we couldn't be overheard. Jewel surreptitiously glanced at our exchange. I'm sure that she was wondering if she might get a clue as to what was eating at her husband.

"It was all settled, right?" I confronted Garland with obvious sarcasm.

"Benny, I tried to catch you before…"

"Before they snapped me?"

"You know how those fellows can be. They're just holding off on your gig. But it's just a bump in the road, friend."

"Garland, in a day, just like that? Just like that at the last moment?" I retorted defiantly, my voice muzzled. I could feel the muscles of my jaws bulging out the sides of my face.

"It's a bump, Benny," Garland nonchalantly slanted the events of the prior day. "Not even a jut or a bulge. It's definitely not a block. It's a bump."

"One more bump…one more bump!"

"There'll be a thousand more opportunities just like this one. Hell, my next *Who's Who* party is coming soon. Can't you see the long road ahead?" Garland pitched to encourage me. "Open your eyes, Benny."

I was in such mental pain that I could barely listen. I

do know that contrary to the prescription of *opening* my eyes suggested by Garland, *closing* them was what I did. I heard the first few bars of "I Close My Eyes" playing in my head. My face dropped into my hands, masking the sorrow that weighed down on me, a deepening gloom, one that Garland remained oblivious to.

Shana took note of my sour temper. "Daddy, what's wrong? Can his little girl perk him up?" she offered coquettishly. I nodded a "no," but the girl was not finished. "Daddy must have had a blah day at work."

Jewel was standing across the room. From a distance, she tried to elicit a response from her man. "Baby, what's wro…"

"Just scowling, Jewel. He gets in his moods," Garland sang out, answering on my behalf.

"I should be celebrating? Look what they did to me," I wearily countered Garland's refusal to appreciate the devastation I was experiencing.

"You're golden. Come on now."

Garland winked at Jewel and took me by the arm, leading me to the front door.

"Jewel. I'm borrowing your man for a while. Stay beautiful like I know you will." Exiting the door, he revealed his plan to lift my spirits. "We're going to Benny's favorite pub for a drink."

It was Shana who shouted out the last words. "Remember, Daddy, all you have to do is close your eyes."

Jewel knew I was in trouble over something but

couldn't imagine what could be so overwhelmingly terrible to evoke an emotional state she'd never before seen in me. She said nothing; instead, she circumspectly eyed our twosome as we walked out the front door.

CHAPTER 4: IT'S GUARANT E E D TO SUCC E E D

Garland was nearly dragging me out of the house. I had no desire to leave, no enthusiasm for visiting Jimbo's, and even less interest in being with Garland, although I lacked the energy or will to resist. I remember stopping as we approached the street. It was dark outside. I twisted around to gaze backward at the house. That's when I felt this odd sensation of disassociation, as if I had no connection with it or anything inside. Worse still, I had the thought that I was never coming back.

At the time, we were living in an area of Detroit called Mexicantown-Southwest. The neighborhood had gone through many changes during the preceding three decades. The community was about fifty percent Hispanic, twenty-five percent African-American, and the rest a variety of Caucasian types, from American to Italian to Hungarian, with even a smattering of Asians.

I mention this ethnic mix because it mirrored the multiplicity of backgrounds of our friends. Even going to my favorite spot to have a beer, Jimbo's, the clientele spanned the globe with different colors, religions, races, cultures, and nationalities. The geographic region itself had become a magnet for people living in the greater Detroit city who wanted an ethnic Mexican food experience. All along Bagley Street and Vernor Highway were clusters of these purported authentic ethnic restaurants.

Garland led me toward Vernor where Jimbo's sat, nestled between several of these eating spots. It was a plain vanilla bar run by a proprietor who generously named his establishment in honor of himself. The business was not a thriving enterprise in terms of making the owner wealthy, but due to the socio-economics of its clientele and its ability to produce a decent revenue stream, it wasn't a dive either.

It was populated by regulars, drawn to the haunt by both the comradeship enjoyed between the patrons and the graciousness of the owner. Jimbo was the type of man who found it difficult to draw the line between his role as a businessman and that of being a friend, confidante, and counselor for the primarily male customers who stopped in for a brief respite from the agony of their lives as worker bees.

As we approached our destination, I glanced into the

window of a closed shop. Reflected from the glass was Garland's figure. He was dressed in a fine cotton shirt under a lightweight silk sport coat. His hair was thick, black, and slick. The short strands curled buoyantly, offering the impression that life was a carnival ride.

What stood out most distinctly for me, however, was the slight bagging beginning to weigh under Garland's eyes. It blemished the otherwise immaculate image of a man I had "known" since we were sandlot buddies. As I consciously reflected on my relationship with him, I concluded that I understood almost nothing about what he believed in or stood for, other than power and wealth.

We kept walking. Garland used the opportunity to pump up the sullen man slouching by his side.

"You gotta keep going, going, going. This business is nothing but highs and lows."

"For me, lows and lowers."

"Well, highs and highers are comin' soon. Smile, Benny, you're right...there."

Garland paused intentionally to separate his last two words. He used the interlude between "right" and "there" to draw my attention to the tiny distance he had measured between his right thumb and index finger.

"For the last three years, you've been my agent and manager and for the last three years I've been *right there!* Garland, it's been most of my life that I've been *right there!*" I emphasized my objection by mimicking Garland's hand gesture.

"Benny Wright, Most Likely To Succeed, Class of '94. You're our hope. I've looked up to you since we were digging in dirt to get to China," he howled.

"Yeah. Tell me about all the guys in our yard who grew up with us. M.D., Ph.D., NFL, NBA, CIA, and C-E-O!" I emphasized the last title while pointing at Garland. "What about The Most Likely To Succeed? Z-E-R-O. Hell, I'm still selling songs for a dime."

"Don't get glum on me. Today don't mean a thing. Don't get droopy-eyed and numb on me. Today don't mean a thing. With the future I see for you; today don't mean a thing."

We had just reached the door to Jimbo's, but before entering I delivered a decisive speech.

"No more, Garland. That family of mine...I've dreamed away their futures." By now, my eyes were droopy and I was on the verge once more of tears. I succeeded in choking down my emotions by deliberately tightening my chest, cheek, and neck muscles. "I'm finished," I proclaimed as much to myself as Garland.

"Your future is starting over, right now!" Garland characteristically dismissed my edict.

Garland opened the door to Jimbo's. It wasn't the familiarity of the smell and friendly faces that startled both of us to silence. I'd prepared a compilation of songs for Jimbo and had put them on a CD. It had been some time since I'd last heard it, but by chance as we stood at the threshold of what Garland knew was a joint where

I enjoyed mixing with the boys, one of my best jazzy sounds was blasting. It was not solely the coincidence of one of his client's tunes being played that animated Garland, it was the particular piece, named "Get Moved."

Garland leapt into the bar, tugging at me and forcing me to follow. As we entered, Garland hollered to me over the music and chatter, loud enough so as to make a public statement, "You know what your problem is?"

"Yeah, I do. That's what I'm trying to explain to you," I shot back petulantly.

"Your problem is you sulk your way through the tough stuff."

Garland heard the sound increasing in intensity and couldn't stop himself.

"I've got a different strategy," he shouted so as to gain the attention of all the men in the bar. "I need to get that lyric back in your heart."

By this time, Garland had succeeded in pausing all the customers from either guzzling their drinks or panting over the game on the large screen televisions that Jimbo had installed around the perimeter of the room. I noticed that my best friend, Craig, and another good friend, Link, were there. In no time, Garland rallied the whole joint to challenge my dejected state, though not one knew what I was "sulking" over.

"Boys, how about encouraging Benny to lay down a line?" Garland called out.

"Come on Benny, give us that line," the crowd shouted.

"Give me a line, Benny," Garland coaxed.

I couldn't be budged out of my funk if they had all been threatening me with rifles, but still, Garland was undeterred.

"I'll get this going," my dear agent volunteered. "I've got lots of lines," he trumpeted delightedly to all the customers gathered around us.

The sound of "Get Moved" rose in volume. Garland began performing the lyrics I had written for the song. Jimbo joined in, followed by Link who performed the final verses. I must admit, they put on quite a show, dancing and jiving, having a grand old time…yet completely oblivious to how I was feeling. I can still hear the chorus and lines that I'd written.

"Move, do it with me, groove, right through it with me; get moved, smile with me tonight."

It repeated several times before Garland stole the stage, intent on nagging me out of my funk.

"Give me a line man, give me a beat. Get hopin' again, feelin' so sweet. All you gotta do is just lean on me, rock with me, fly with me. What's it gonna take for me to get you loud, risin' again with that passion roused? Benny baby, don't die on me, just love the drive and love the dream."

He had no intention of backing off. Instead, he reached his hand around my neck, pulling me close to him.

"Give me a hug. I'll rub off some hope and some love.

There's no need to shrug, we'll get that magic back so don't you crack, just like that. Benny baby, you know I love to see you get w-i-l-d. Benny baby, you know I love to see you get riled up. So come on now, get moved and smile with me tonight."

The sound continued. It was Jimbo that picked up the next verse.

"Damn it Benny, don't get down on me, not when I'm tappin' a keg and it's free. Do what you need to get up, and get out of this rut. Come on, let's toast to Ben, glasses up for a real good friend, the legend, Magic, we love you 'til the end."

The entire group of customers was having a ball. It was like they were all clowns singing together on stage.

"Move, do it with me. Groove right through it with me. Get moved, smile with me tonight," they entreated my hapless soul.

Finally, Jimbo turned down the music, but the beat continued in the background.

I'd describe Jimbo's as a tame neighborhood bar where most of the people came more to socialize then to get drunk, although there were a few who considered alcohol to be a career. As the interior went silent, Link, Craig and Garland stood in the center of the room with me next to them.

"Garland, Garland. Strange to see you in a dive like this," Link teased. He draped his arm over Craig's shoulder. "Did Benny tell you what the two of us have got in the works? You'll never hear anything quite so sexy." Link smiled as he placed his hand over his heart. "But we won't show you a thing without a contract."

Both Link and Craig had the music bug too. They were singing and writing partners in their spare time, trying to get their gig together, although they had less of a chance than I did.

"Benny, you look like...death," Craig said with concern, now honing in on my depressive state.

"He's down on life boys. Benny's planning to quit on his music career, just like that," Garland informed them while snapping his fingers to highlight his point.

Hearing the statement, Jimbo abruptly cut the music. "Uh, uh, not in Jimbo's he isn't," he asserted from behind the bar.

I stood gazing at my surroundings. One of the alluring features of Jimbo's was that while it was a middle-class joint, it had a feeling of dignity. The interior was crafted primarily from several types of wood. Most outstanding to my eye was the bar itself, which stood toward the rear of the large room. It was long and arched at the ends to abut the wall.

The bar top was beautiful, the chestnut wood accented by a marbling pattern that reminded me of a prime Spencer steak. The rest of the structure was made from intricately detailed mahogany. There were numerous drawers and racks atop for hanging glasses of varying shapes and sizes. The back was mirrored and covered with bottles of hard liquor. The piece spoke of durability and a symbol of assurance to the customers that it would be there dispensing spirits long after they'd taken their last shot.

Jimbo took pride in maintaining his establishment, though the floor, composed of planks of dark walnut, spoke to wear and tear visible even under the dim lighting. The inside was painted a tan color, but around the perimeter of the ceiling a thin strip of orange accented the otherwise plain walls.

The unlikely silence after Jimbo turned off my beat pricked the attention of everyone in the bar. A man I recognized but didn't know by name, one of the customers who drank heavily, dropped off the chair where he was sitting and strolled up to me. Pantomiming, he took a stethoscope out of his pocket and held it to my heart.

"J. C. in heaven, it's not movin'," the man jested after lingering over my organ for a few seconds.

His act completed, he stumbled back to his drink that was resting on a nearby table. He faced the basketball game projecting from the large-screen television and called to me.

"Come on over here, Benny, and watch my Detroit Pistons in action. Let Jimbo get you on track for the hi-i-life and tomorrow you won't remember a thing," the man blathered jovially.

"I always remember," countered one of the other more

lighthearted customers sitting near the man. "That's why I keep coming back."

"If I had to wake up to your wife, I'd always come back too," the drunk taunted.

"You do always come back. What's your excuse?" the man questioned while gulping a large volume from a beer mug.

"My wife is uglier than yours…and meaner," he jived.

"Benny, you…quitting? But it all felt so right," Craig said, rescuing me from the antics of the drunks.

"Yes, yes, yes, Craig. It was perfectly right for Benny Wright, Biggest Fool, Class of '94. I'm failing everyone. Blowing bubbles of fantasy to hide in."

"Well, then until you blow another one, at least honor us with one last performance," Link urged just as Jimbo hit the button to start the music again.

Jimbo was pouring glasses, ranting joyfully. "Look at these classy customers that I have to tend to and this kid's talking about givin' up. Nobody gives up at Jimbo's."

That's all I can recall until much later that night. It seems during my time at the bar, I drifted into a mental state where I lost complete track of myself. I can earnestly state that I don't remember a thing after the singing of "Get Moved," until Jimbo called out, "Last round, team. Jimbo's going home."

By then, there were still several customers in the place, but Garland, Craig, and Link had already left. I don't know how I blanked it all out. While there would

49

be numerous occasions during ensuing weeks when I'd take excursions beyond my normal awareness, with or without the aid of alcohol, I'm certain that up to this point in the evening I didn't even have one single drink.

Jimbo was wiping the counter. He seemed to be in a talkative state.

"Benny, it'll be okay. We've heard your sound, we've loved your beats, and you'll conquer."

"I had so many opportunities that I passed up for this pipe dream. What did I do to my family?" I muddled my words, spoken to nobody in particular.

"Your family? You're doing everything right. Right boys?" Jimbo inquired of the remaining drinkers.

There was definitely a zany humor to the scene. Jimbo kept calling out, "Right boys?" and in unison the inebriated late-night clients replied back perfunctorily, "Right, Jimbo."

"You're fighting for something better," Jimbo offered. "Every other man I know seems to be fighting for something worse. Let me tell you my story," Jimbo said, motioning for me to sit closer. "One time, a while ago, I had a wife and children too. And on top of that, a damn good job to support 'em...right boys?"

"Right, Jimbo," the chorus replied.

"But for every night you've spent with a headphone on one side of your head or another, I spent with a pretty young thing on either side of me. Well, eventually my wife caught me. She dropped me, kicked me out, and left me in the street where I belonged…right boys?"

"Right, Jimbo."

"By that point, with my fightin' so hard to ruin everything, my becoming a thing of the past was the best deal for all of us. They were all better off, way better off! My whole family thrived without me…right boys?"

"Right, Jimbo."

I couldn't help flashing back to the dying man, seeing his face and hearing his words. Then, listening to the inane disclosure by Jimbo somehow struck a chord with me. Things like that can happen when a mind is suffering. A person can become vulnerable to believe in the most tangled and idiotic forms of reason. They can even conclude that the thoughts they had to reach a conclusion were conceived from a majestic logic that couldn't have been calculated with any normal state of reason. They credit themselves with having stepped out of the proverbial box and hitting on a gem of a solution to their problem. Even more dangerous is that there is a tendency to embrace the ill-conceived plan as if sanctioned by The Man above. The person then refuses any pleas of sound intellect to drop the nonsensical approach they're advocating.

On this particular night, after all that had transpired, Jimbo's disclosure included, I thought that I had just hatched "The Perfect Plan."

"It will be the best thing for everyone," I recall stating out loud, as if rehearsing prayer.

"Right, Benny. We all blame it on ourselves when things tumble in our family, but that's how us men are wired," Jimbo philosophized. "You're free now, Benny, free. And that's the best thing for everyone."

I was hardly paying attention at this point. Instead, I was reflecting on an idea that kept flickering on and off in a closet of my mind. It caused me to pause, but it was only for the smallest fraction of a second, just sufficient for me to designate myself a genius.

"Jimbo, I think you may have stumbled on to something."

The bar was silent except for the sound of Jimbo washing glasses and the chattering of the remaining customers as they paid up their tabs. In that silence, I heard music. It was a spirited beat extraordinaire; it was the type of creation of sound that came to me at moments of grace, gifts dropped from heaven.

I noticed on this occasion that the notes were emanating out of a sweet vision. I fondled it. As I did, the elements of the musical piece came popping out at an accelerated pace. I stood up. Words spontaneously floated out of my mouth. A feeling of lightness came over me. I recall experiencing the weight of dust. I had found redemption for the pain I'd put my family and myself through—there was hope. Hell, my method was "Guarant e e d to Succ e e d." I called out to Jimbo.

"Hold on, wait a second. You got it right, and I got a plan. This little plan, oh it feels so right, perfectly packed and wrapped up tight."

I was on a roll, spinning out lyrics as if I *was* Magic.

"It's a beautiful, beautiful thing, and it called me so quick with a beautiful ring. Oh, Jewel, you don't know how I feel. I can get you caressed but I can't get you a meal. Now I got that fantasy life, all packed up and it's comin' tonight. Jewel, can you hear me?" I wailed. "A little bit of luxury is alright, a little bit of diamonds, a little less plight, a little bit of piles of gold, a little Bentley and an SUV, a little trip from the cold. A little bit's nice, a little bit's nice," I repeated joyfully, "when it's a little bit of everything you wanted in life. Can you see it? A little bit of a mansion, a little bit of Van Gogh, a little bit of a landing in a place called Cabo."

I was convinced I had a winner and voiced no shame as I sung it out. "It's guarant e e d to succ e e d. Just believe in me, come on believe in me. It's guarant e e d to succ e e d…if things work just the way I see." I paused with a smile, charmed by my own message. "Just like the days pass quick and become the past, and the spring-time blooms the summertime grass. Ladies want love, no questions asked, and it always draws a fight when the dream gets crashed."

Was I talking to Jewel, Jimbo, the customers in the bar, the whole of mankind or only myself? I had no idea, but my enthusiasm kept words slipping off my tongue like baby drool.

"Just like a dude like you gets boozed, and a guy like me gets rocked and refused, a lucky man, he'll get the world on a spoon, with a cherry on top 'til he ages on prunes. It's a matter of a fact I got this plan locked up, a smile on my face and I'm about to erupt. It couldn't be more guaranteed, so long as everything works out perfectly."

The beat kept playing in my head, but the volume softened. I was certain about what had taken place. It was unmistakable. Benny Wright, a man who would denounce religious zealots while still maintaining a basic faith in God, had been the subject of an official Epiphany, delivered by a greater power, calling him to be a transformed person—one blissful in a state of everlasting peace, forgiveness, and atonement.

That's when it hit me. The last words of the dying young man: "Sometimes we have to do the right thing, even if we die..." Then Jimbo's comment: "It was the best thing for everyone."

It hadn't been by random chance that I happened upon the murder. I was there to receive instruction, divine providence; the prescription to do the right thing even though it might kill me. The bar owner's companion statement reinforced what I had just that moment concluded.

Jimbo stared at me like a puffed up poppa whose

son homered in the bottom of the ninth inning to win a ballgame.

"You got it!" Jimbo complimented me, unaware what had transpired for his customer.

"I'll get them everything I promised."

"You'll do it, Benny!"

"It's guaranteed," I smiled confidently to Jimbo.

My initial jubilant state—even the music itself having been born out of elation in the moment of enlightenment—was, however, to be seasoned by the time-ticking sobering fingers of reality, ones that were not rapping on my psyche that evening at Jimbo's.

I refused then, and for some time thereafter, to revisit an old maxim I knew to be "guaranteed." The principle states that there are only two things one can absolutely count on in life—we all know what they are, death and taxes. I must have thought I could beat the system. Sadly, I had just invested my life savings in a penny stock and thought I had bought shares in Coca Cola.

CHAPTER 5: GOING HOME

My home was located on the corner of Campbell and Merritt Streets. It practically butted up to the easterly neighbor's house, but the western side offered a wide grassy space where one of the pair of giant ash trees resided. It was a quarter after two in the morning when I arrived, frightfully late for a wife accustomed to her husband never staying out past nine without forewarning her of some commitment.

My eyes were blurry and my head was whirling by the time I reached my corner. After my prophetic vision guaranteeing that my problems were solved, I had guzzled several drinks in celebration. I was usually a man who was respected for drinking socially but never to excess. However, that night I was excited and decided I deserved a reward for concocting a plan of action I knew was the ultimate answer to my dilemma.

I lay on the grassy side of my property for a while before a chill brought me partially to my senses. When I tried to stand, I fell back to the ground. It took three tries to lift up my frame so I could walk clumsily toward the house.

The façade of my home was grey brick. The first half of the walk up to the house was on a concrete path that widened slightly before it transitioned to a long cement stairway with an iron balustrade that ended at the balcony. I don't know when our home had been built, but I'm certain it was well over a hundred years old, the most reliable confirmation of that fact being the undulating wear and tear on the front steps and the steel posts that revealed, at random locations, the application of innumerable layers of varying colors of paint.

That evening when I reached the railing to make my way up the stairs, my poor balance became all the more evident. I grabbed hold to steady my swaying body. The lights were on in the living room. As I opened the door, there was Jewel, sitting in her chair with an open book on her lap. She didn't move. She stared at her husband, frozen from action by conflicting feelings of relief and rage.

Finally, she stood. The bitterness she had swallowed from the thought of what I must have been up to out-dueled the inclination toward a benefit-of-the-doubt approach, especially since she witnessed a smirk stretch across my face. Her jaw flexed as she gritted her teeth, pointing at the wall clock, as if she had convicted the timekeeping device as a serial murderer. It read only a few lousy minutes before two-thirty; it was by then April 17th.

"Where have you been? It's 2:30 in the morning. You walk in with a grin at 2:30 a.m.?"

"Come on, you're no fun. I've been partying."

I grabbed an umbrella out of a large tin container near the front door where we stored several similar ones. I walked over close to Jewel, opening the device to canopy both of us, as if we were standing in a storm.

"And what is it you're rejoicing over?" Jewel asked indignantly.

"It's done. I worked it out. See, your guy has a plan. No, I mean your *man* has a plan!"

"Well, Benny, my man, you better leave me out of the plan."

"Oh, no, no. You *are* the plan…you and the children. And don't you ever forget it." I stumbled across the room, my fractured words burning on Jewel like pellets of acid rain.

I walked into the kitchen and opened the refrigerator. There were two cans of beer, and I took one, still holding the umbrella. Jewel ran over to grab the can out of my hand.

"Are you some sort of fool?"

"No, Jewel, I've become some sort of a…not fool," I giggled…foolishly.

58

"Look at me. Stop!" she whispered with a harsh tone, soft enough so as not to wake the children but forceful enough to ensure that I got the point. She grabbed at my arms to force me to stand still and face her. "I'm going to keep asking, so tell me what's got you by the horns, Benny, my love?"

"Nothing at all. I'm just a changed man," I gloated.

"That I can see," she assured me. Then half-pleading and half-threatening, she added, "Just don't let this happen again."

I couldn't contain my excitement. As I fell backward into my favorite chair, my face unabashedly giddy in appearance, I answered ingratiatingly, "Yes, dear."

Then I fell asleep in the chair. As was the case after the night of the murder, I woke up and went to work in the morning. Following my shift, I stopped off at Jimbo's, where I drank myself silly before returning home—this went on for the next two evenings.

Jewel waited up but didn't say a word until the third installment of late-night misbehavior. Then things turned nasty. By that point, she'd concluded I was deliberately tormenting her. She complained about the cruelty of my actions, a mean madness she'd never imagined possible from me—like I'd become a demon. Making matters worse, she was exhausted after not being able to sleep since the night of the murder. She had cried and pleaded each time she was with me, but I was insensitive to her suffering. In the past, I had always been tender and attentive, but now I ignored her and the children as well.

"Benny, I'm going to ask you one more time why you're doing this to us," Jewel voiced in a demanding tone. "You're doing it on purpose, aren't you?"

Her plea earned nothing from me besides my nearly passing out on the sofa.

"Damn you! Damn you for whatever it is you're doing, Benny," she shouted loud enough to wake the children as well as alarm the neighbor next door.

"You just got to learn to let things flow, darlin'," I finally answered from my inebriated state.

"Oh, you've become a master at flowing…in your ocean of liquor."

I responded with what she later recalled as an eerie hypnotic rhythm to my words. "Oh, but just wait 'til I get to where I'm flowing. Just wait 'til I flow away. You got to know when to let me flow…when it's the only way." Then I stood and began snapping my fingers as I spoke. "Hey, hey, you gotta learn to let me flow when it's the only way…to go."

I could see my jesting and lack of sensitivity bringing her to a cold freeze. She thawed instantly, breaking down in tears; her feeling jackknifing back and forth, disbelief to terror and back to astonishment. I was the man of her life, forever, no matter what. Whatever I was suffering, if I thought it was going to take her down, break her spirit so she'd quit on her love for me, she was there to assure me I was mistaken.

I had written music and lyrics that covered just about every known condition and circumstance of mankind and a few added ones that I'd invented on my own. Over the years, she'd heard me play them repeatedly and knew almost every word I'd composed. This one song, one of my best love ballads, "Staying Right Here with You," came to her mind. She jumped in my face and shouted, "Listen, god damn it!"

I have to admit, it was the best I'd ever heard the song done.

"Lovin' ain't an easy thing, most people can't do it right, but I long for you like a fairy tale so we better give it one good try. You run from me and punish me, and I couldn't even tell you why, so come back to me, back in peace and live with a painted smile. Benny, I remember days we'd pray to lay away in bed, but lately all you pray to do is liquor up instead."

Jewel is a fiery woman. If my plan was guaranteed to succeed, I realized as I listened to her that I'd be challenged at every turn.

"What happened to the magic in your name, the passion you had for fame, the fire in your lungs that would shoot out warmth when the winter came? You make me fight, when I just want a gentle touch, a little warming sign. You make me cry when I just wanna cuddle with you through the night, and feel I'm fine. You make these stands when I just wanna lay you down and let you feel my love. But I'm stayin' right here with you, 'cause I care and it's true, it's you and me, me and you."

Her eyes watered as she forced me to look directly at her.

"I could never tell you that I know about the pain you feel inside, but open up a little and I swear to you this, I'll battle it down in size. Surround me with the hurt you feel, let me feel it too, but don't go stabbin' away, and givin' me my own damn open wounds. It's too damn late to drive me away, too damn stupid to drink through pain, too damn selfish to give up a dream of love, but I'm here, I just wish you wouldn't make me fight."

Her final words, "You make me fight," she shot out like a heavyweight jab. I flinched for a second. I stood weak-kneed, staring at her. For the first time, I thought that the shadow of my love had devoured my perfect plan and left me standing naked. Fortunately, I was able to recompose quickly. I delivered a mere three words, but I knew they were infuriating to her.

"You don't understand."

"Why should I?" Jewel yelled as she ran tearfully to our bedroom.

I was sadly aware of how much I was hurting her but believed by then that I had no choice but to dispense "tough love." I had envisioned a plan. It was perfect, guaranteed to succeed, and Jewel and the children might suffer in the short run but in the end, they would respect and appreciate what I had done for them.

Had I become some sort of non-fool? Everyone will have the honor to judge that for themselves, on their own terms. I'm certain of one thing, now that the affair has played out—I had guts, determination, and a belief that I was doing right. One might be inclined to counter that statement, even without hearing the rest of my story, by noting that so did most madmen.

But in fairness, I had love, the deepest and most devout; mine was unmitigated, unbounded, and unlimited. That gave me the strength to let Jewel have her pity-party—all she wanted of them. It mattered not; her man was going to get her everything he "knew" she wanted and needed.

CHAPTER 6: CRUSHING DREAMS

While all the fun and games were playing out at the Wright home, where was my devoted representative, Garland? At Jimbo's, of course. Yeah, he was a high-class dude who typically flashed himself at the most prestigious establishments in our home city, but he could never rinse the grit out of his underwear. Garland, on some level, knew he was a street boy who belonged with the troops in the trenches. Thus, when the opportunity presented itself, he'd escape to our local saloon where he could take off his coat and tie and use his shirtsleeve as a Kleenex. On this particular afternoon, he was sitting at the bar with a pile of documents in front of him and a beer just to his right, intently focused on reading the material, when his cell chimed.

"Garland here," he answered in his exuberantly staged voice.

He waited a second for the caller to reveal his identity. "I know he's top of the line, and now he's all mine. Yep." He paused again while the person explained the reason for his call. Then Garland addressed the point. "Oh, Magic'll survive; business is business. Out with the old, in with the new. No shame; it's the name of the game," he gaily rhymed, followed by several repeated, signature ha-ha chuckles. "And I'll still throw Magic a bone now and again 'cause he's my brother from a different mother."

Garland hadn't finished his conversation when his secretary, Georgia, rushed in. The lady was tall and slender—her long, bright red hair flowed straight down off her head like molten lava. The woman possessed no walking gear. Instead, she waddled at a brisk pace, no doubt a nervous habit since simultaneous with her penguin-type walk, she constantly jerked her neck right and left as if she were a fugitive.

When Garland spotted her, he sensed trouble. "Hold on a minute," he spoke into the phone.

Georgia, with her typical histrionic style of exaggerated expressions and gestures, began to talk in a pant even before she reached her boss. "Link and Craig were waiting two hours at the office; honey, they were ready to camp out in the lobby."

"They weren't on my calendar, right?"

"I swear, darling, they just pranced right in like you

were expecting a special delivery." Georgia let her sweet southern accent testify to her innocence.

"Every time they bump into me they start thinking… Georgia, just tell them I got held up; we'll get back to them."

"Well, you see…there's a slight problem. I made a little mistake," Georgia fluttered. "They asked me where you were and I told them you…might be having a meeting at…"

"You told them I was here?"

"No, I mean, not exactly," Georgia explained, stumbling over her words. "They just figured it out and then said they were coming right over, so I rushed out ahead of them to warn you."

"Okay, just hold on," Garland halted her. Then he addressed the party waiting for him on the phone. "Looks like I've got a couple other Magics I need to dispose of…a little spring cleaning, friend. These old hacks'll break your back," he divined gregariously. "I'll call you when I got something hot, 'cause I know you can't be caught on a long shot soon to be forgot." Laughing boisterously, he then finished off the conversation. "Okay, bye, bye."

Georgia was frantic about the way the incident might play out. She widened her arms to accentuate the question. "Well?"

"Hell, let's get it over with. When they get here, I'll see them for a minute and get rid of them," he informed her, but with notable irritation for my two friends were famous for pestering Garland every chance they had.

Only a few seconds passed before the front door opened. It was three in the afternoon and the twosome of Craig and Link, who normally would have never shown up at that hour, waltzed in. Due to a parts shortage, their shift had been cancelled. Both men made a straight line for Garland. As Link enthusiastically raised his arm to high-five Garland, Georgia intercepted his hand with hers. Instead of an earnest slap, Link, caught off-guard by her zany interference, halfheartedly tapped her hand. At the same time, his facial expression appeared stunned by her audaciousness, her unexpected attempt to display, and then impose, herself into a man's custom.

Garland was standing. When the men reached him, he engaged in ceremonial shakes, hugs, and smiles like they were his best buddies.

"Looking up, looking good," Garland greeted them.

Georgia stepped to the side, a spectator to the surreal scene unfolding.

"My man! Show us the dotted line…we're ready to sign," Craig clowned.

"You all are right…there." Garland had lots of signature gestures. One of his favorites, however, was the one he'd used on me, narrowing the space between his fingers to let his eager subjects know they were on the verge of a breakthrough.

"You've been behind us all the way." Link said. "This time we're gonna blow you away."

He was holding a CD. He extended his arm so Garland could see it.

"Can't wait, can't wait, but...what a day," Garland replied with a step backward. "Things are locked tight, so if you just leave that with me, I'll listen up tonight."

"You got to hear this. I mean we've been waiting hours," Link persisted.

"I wish to god I could, but..."

"It's got it all. Our heart, our soul, our story; our ups and downs," Craig chimed in to further the pitch.

"All wrapped up in one track," Link boasted.

"It's our anthology...it is moneymaking music," Craig forcefully asserted.

Garland relented, but didn't let his lack of enthusiasm go unnoticed. "Sure, but..."

"You'll see. It's a new Link and Craig," the team heralded. "Wait until we kick this for you. Then see if you want to knock us down."

Jimbo had been in and out of the bar area during the encounter but was missing at the moment he was needed to power up the music player. Link inserted the disc on his own.

"This is everything we have, Garland," Link twittered as the music began.

"We can't take another knockout blow," Craig said as the song entitled "T.K.O." began.

The two performers smiled proudly at one another. Link pointed to Garland as he hollered over the increasing sound of the beat. "Damn, Garland, this is the goods."

From the onset of the performance, Georgia tried to focus on the team, nodding approvingly when she had the chance. But Garland insisted on hogging her attention, tapping her on the shoulder to direct her to some of the papers he had scattered on the counter.

"Garland!" Craig shouted at one point, noticing he wasn't listening.

"I've been behind you all the way," Garland mindlessly assured them, not even looking in their direction. "Now's the moment to groove it fellows."

By this time Jimbo—to whom I owe my knowledge of these details, since I didn't have the opportunity to witness this event firsthand—came into the room. In recounting the story, he assured me that Garland had been engaged in everything *but* giving an eye to the boys or an ear to the music.

"It was sad," Jimbo said dolefully. "He looked over papers with Georgia and then lingered on the damn phone. He wouldn't even glance at them. He even turned to me partway through his phone call and said a few words, but the sound of the music was so loud that whatever he was trying to convey got muffled. Then he went back to the conversation on his cell. Finally, he hung up. But even then, rather than watch the boys, he scanned the material in front of him again, forcing his secretary to do the same. Finally, he signed a couple of letters that Georgia had brought with her."

The bartender shook his head several times. "It was terrible. They were so hot. The lyrics and the beat—it was one of the best performances I've ever seen."

Link started the piece, alternating verses with Craig.

"I take knockout blows, blow after blow 'til I'm knocked out cold."

"I take knockout blow after blow, blow after blow and I won't let go. Blow after blow 'til I'm knocked out cold and I won't let go 'til I'm TKO'd."

"I remember the day when I was a young boy lookin' to play. With a microphone, I was all alone, my friends couldn't get in my way. I wanted to sing out in songs. I wanted to bring out the throngs. So I trained myself strong.

"I grew and my music did too, to a level that it never knew, to the point that I couldn't just stop 'til I opened the world to my tunes. So I introduced the things I did to the ones I knew, let 'em hear it through, and tell me what they wanted to. Well, they said that I'm better than great, and they told me not to hesitate. So I did just that and twenty years quickly passed, always close…then slash!

"No, we can't go on takin' knockout blows, it hurts too much inside our souls, we can't take another T.K.O."

I couldn't believe the song when I later heard it. I

might as well have written it because it was my life they were describing. Craig handled the next lines alone.

"So they always said, work enough and get the bread. Well, I worked ten to ten for twenty years to pay my rent. How does that seem, like an American dream? It makes me scream. But I get back on in 'cause those bigwigs shake on my hand with a grin. Well, I'm the guy who puts his life out on the line, and takes the hits straight to the spine...and tastes the grime."

Together they wrapped it up. "But we can't go on takin' knockout blows, it hurts too much inside our souls, we can't take another T.K.O."

"Guys," Garland called out after they completed their performance. "Guys!"

The music quieted. Jimbo clapped and then went back to get supplies from the storage room.

"Yeah! See what you can do with that," Craig and Link challenged Garland—their parting gesture.

"I'll get back to you. Later, fellas," Garland informed them matter-a-fact.

The two then walked out. Garland responded to his ringing cell phone again. Georgia interrupted him.

"Hold on," he said into the phone before turning to Georgia. "Well?" he said to his secretary.

"Well, what?" She jerked backward with widened eyes.

'Well, Jewel told me you're a stick of dynamite... and you want to learn the biz, right?" Garland asked, reminding her that it was because of Georgia's best friend, my wife, Jewel, that he had hired her.

"You bet. I dream of it every night," she responded passionately.

Garland moved close to her, speaking right up to her ear. "So now, be a doll, go back to the office and then in an hour or so call Craig and Link and tell them it's a no-go."

"A no-go? Just like that? But didn't you hear them?" she rapped at him in her thick accent that more often than not was unintentionally humorous. Then she mimicked verses from Craig and Link's performance to be sure Garland had heard their message. "They can't go on takin' knockout blows, it hurts too much inside their souls. They can't take another...T...K...O."

"Welcome to the industry," Garland beamed, inducting her like a recruit.

"Hot damn!" Georgia uttered, befuddled. "But..."

"No room for tender hearts here. Dear, they'll keep fighting even if it kills them...these people never know when to hang it up. Besides, who am I to say miracles never come true?"

Georgia walked out. Her head was bobbing. The lady too dazed to speak. While she was on her way out, Garland's cell was working non-stop.

"Garland here." His greeting was robust, full of delight. "Yeah, just got through with a meeting, but listen. Now, be patient. I'm behind you all the way. Wait for the break." He paused. "Whoops, I got another call...I gotta go."

Garland slipped on his coat and looked in the mirror behind the bar. He stared at himself with great contentment. Then he tightened his tie, straightened it, puffed out his chest, and headed for the exit door.

"I thought Benny might be coming by," he said to Jimbo. "When you see him, tell him I'll catch him up later tonight."

CHAPTER 7: A HEART IN THE RIGHT PLACE

I recall the evening I dropped in at Jimbo's and heard Craig and Link's tale. There were no customers when I arrived. I had nothing to do that day, so I offered to help Jimbo put some beers in the refrigerator under the counter. He started chatting while he passed bottles for me to store.

"Um, um. It was awful, Benny," Jimbo began the story. "They sang their hearts out, right here at Jimbo's. After they finished, I heard Garland tell that secretary of his… um, um…he could have cared less what Craig and Link did; they never had a chance."

Jimbo, of course, was referring to Craig and Link having performed "T. K. O." for Garland the previous afternoon. While Jimbo was narrating for me much of what I've already reported about Craig and Link's performance, Craig arrived. He looked wretched; Garland's rejection was weighing unpleasantly on his temperament.

"Jimbo, drink," Craig muttered dispiritedly.

"You got it. You're not doing so good," Jimbo observed with compassion.

"Feel like my lights got shut off."

"Sorry, Craig. I just heard," I commiserated.

"Already? How could you already know?" Craig posed.

"A little birdie told him," Jimbo said playfully.

Link strode in at that moment. In contrast to Craig, his mood appeared elevated, and he began to speak before he took a seat.

"Hey, Benny, I wrote a new song and this one's got gold and platinum oozing out of it."

Craig looked at his partner with a mocking stare. "Yeah, you know, Link, I think I just heard it on the radio on my way over."

"I wrote this one for you, Benny," he said exuberantly, completely ignoring Craig's moaning.

"Sorry, Link, that song's not gonna ever have my voice on it."

"Sounds like it's going to be a smash," Craig added sarcastically.

"With Benny, it will. Right now, Benny, you're a true artist." Link reflected and then answered the obvious question he expected me to pose. "Why is that the case?

Because, Benny, you can touch people where they're feeling the deepest, where they're struggling the most."

Several other patrons had arrived by this time and taken seats. Others would show up during the discussion that was about to take place. They were all listening to Link, likely surprised that a man known to typically promote a boyish, fun-loving attitude had renounced his customary lightweight persona in favor of a mature enthusiasm—still, they were captivated by his words, ones frothing as if delivered by a speaker at a labor rally.

"This piece I wrote last night is about breaking through monotony," Link summarized for his audience. "The average man toils every rotten day of his life, in and out, at some repetitive job that leads him nowhere other than his grave."

"I'll drink to that," a bald-headed man, referred to as "Curly," cheered as he lifted his beer bottle. The other men followed his lead and confirmed their appreciation for the sad insight offered by Link.

Curly was followed by an unidentified voice filled with doleful resignation, his words rising out of the general clamor of the patrons. "We're grunts; we know it."

His admission earned another broad applause followed by a collective response from the other men. "We'll drink to that."

"Grunts can take it, right?" Curly proclaimed. "Isn't that what the guy said in that movie? 'That's why they call us grunts, because a grunt can take it, a grunt can take anything.'"

"Curly, it was Platoon, you loon. You don't know nothin'," a customer the men had nicknamed Finch teased.

"Point still made, Finch," an emaciated-appearing man, sitting alone in the corner, called out. "We are grunts, like an army of men fighting for nothing but our survival. Hell. Who cares if we live 'cept maybe the old lady."

"Shit. I come in here to listen to a ballgame, have a shot or two, and buy the courage to go home and be squawked at by my wife and children. You boys are getting too heavy for old Emanuel."

"That's the attitude that inspired my song. Too many of us don't have the will left to stand up," Link shot back at Emanuel's shallow-minded perspective.

A large fellow wearing a sport coat and slacks, Luke, rose as if he was about to step up to the podium. "Gentlemen, Link is trying to say something. Have a drink, but don't forget that most of us are poor bastards who aren't going to get a fair slice of the pie if we don't collect ourselves together and demand more. All over the world, the few rich people have everything and the rest are destitute. But this is America. If we can't have decent lives here, the whole world will lose hope. Damn it, men, we are battling for more than just ourselves."

It was the first time I'd ever witnessed the crowd at

Jimbo's communicating about anything that wasn't related to a sporting event...or sex.

"It all sounds great. Inspirational speech, Luke," countered a man who in one gulp had just downed a mug of beer. "But let's get real. What tools do we have to defend ourselves? You say *together* we have more power. We can't stand up as one because we have nothing to unify us...yeah, for a few who still have it there's hope, but hope buys you a dream crashed. We have no real glue... and we have no weapons."

"That's where you're wrong," Link argued with an unprecedented vehemence. "We do have a weapon. It's ours, a homegrown arsenal, and we love it. The only problem is we keep selling it to our overseers for pennies, allowing them to use it as their atomic bomb to subjugate us..."

"That's a big word, Link," a voice yelled out comically.

Link was worked up and ignored the man. "They're using it to take us down, keep us out of the game."

"What is our weapon? Gonna tell us?" The same man tried to rouse the crowd with a disruptive sneer.

"That's what I've been trying to get at all along. I told you, Benny has the gift to touch people where they feel, where they struggle, in their hearts. We've all felt it. Right, fellows?" Link knew the answer. The silence allowed him to proceed uninterrupted. "It's music! That's our power, our ace in the hole. It's born in our cheap houses. Then we raise it on our crummy streets. But it's the only thing we have that makes us a force, that makes our voice heard, that inspires us to be more than mere grunts."

"Link, a political activist? I never would have guessed it," Craig speculated. The new image of his partner perked him out of his funk. "What do you have in mind for us?"

"It's what I realized last night, after Mr. Hot Shit, Garland, dismissed us. I'm going to inspire the working man of America, give him a sound that belongs to him… that he *can* use to revolt against oppression."

I never saw anything like it. Link picked up two empty bottles and started tapping them on the counter, creating a rhythm. Then he pulled out a CD with a track on it, flipping it to Jimbo who knew that his role was to play it up. It was pure instrumental.

The piece began with the slow beating of a metal-brush swishing sound. Then pipes were introduced, followed by a mix of xylophone and vibraphone instrumentation, leading up to a burst of brass horns. It was in pentatonic scale, and as the pace quickened and cymbals joined in, it seemed there was a call-to-arms. The piece conveyed a driving, marching rhythm, and as each of the iterations unfolded, it commanded determination, discipline, order, and resolution to anyone listening.

The music vibrated out of Jimbo's speakers. It spawned what I interpreted to be a mesmeric state, so strong that customers began following Link's lead. His song had incited them to employ whatever items they could—glasses, bottles, ashtrays, wood and plastic mixing sticks, a broom handle, foot of a barstool, drink coasters, metal rings on their fingers, and their own shoes—and use them as instruments to keep up with the quickening of the beat.

But it was the next phase of the experience that was most astonishing. The men instinctively started to move in synchronized patterns, as if they were gradually becoming an organic mass made of human parts. The sound elevated further and without benefit of a professional choreographer, the customers organized themselves in coordinated dance steps.

To round out the performance, as if they were automatons engaged in repetitive tasks similar to what they might be assigned in a factory assembly line, they tossed back and forth between themselves, like manufactured parts being hand-processed from one employee to another, the objects they had previously used as substitutes for real musical instruments.

I was overwhelmed by what I observed but I never participated, my mind still focused on how I would implement my perfect plan. What I did do was stand expressionless in the dead center of the room while all the amateur actors performed their roles around my immobile body. Finally, the song ended on a hard stop by the drums. All the men raised their right arms in a unified gesture of authority—Link had made his point.

But there was still a dissenting voice, a sole pragmatist intent on shattering the celebration.

"That's all fine and dandy, but I have to lay down a note of reality for you dreamers. Remember the French Revolution, the Russian Revolution, and every other uprising by common folks in the majority? What really happened? Christ, you're all fools. Sure, a few bigwigs ended up with slit throats or heads severed, but in the end…same old, same old. Same old formula, guys; there were a few rich, but the masses remained poor—two percent of the Russian people who fought and died for a dream ended up part of 'The Party.' A crummy two-percent," he nipped at the nonsensical idealists. "They dined on caviar with bottles of champagne earned by selling the nation's black treasure while the rest of the people paled from starvation. They accomplished nothing other than to repeat mankind's idiotic experiment of trying to achieve equality." He waved his hand dismissively to the group and sat down.

"We're not talking about a damn revolution. All we want is a sliver more," Luke answered.

"Doesn't work like that, fellow," the same man rose again to enlighten the doubter. "Rich never have and never will part with a penny they don't have to—that's why they're rich," he bellowed. "The rich are always going to be rich and the poor will always be poor—always been that way and always will be," he paused long enough for the words to settle in. "I believe that's the real point made in that movie."

"So we should just give up, accept it and live like slaves?" Luke argued.

"If you have the courage to face the truth and live it, there's nothing to give up because there's nothing to gain in the first place. Go fight! Get yourself beat up. Then, in the end you'll be right back here at Jimbo's taking down suds with your buddies. That's all you want or expect from life, and if you admit it to yourself you'll be a contented man...for yourself and your family." Once more he sat, this time for good.

The patrons lost interest after the man's dismal perspective sunk in. His version seemed a more believable reality. They meandered back to their seats at tables or the bar, mindlessly focused on the ballgame, leaving Craig and Link with me in the center of the room.

"Screw that bastard; damn coward who doesn't know what he's saying," Link spit. "Fellows, sometimes we have to fight for what we believe is right, even if it might kill us. Now tell me, Benny, 'cept for that hopeless soul, how's that for lifting up your spirit?" Link posed to me, the only man in the room who hadn't moved during the dancing. "It puts me on a high. You know, Benny, I realized that sometimes you're called on to do something and you have no choice but to take the risk, no matter how large it might be."

I couldn't believe what he was saying. So close was

his statement to that of the dying man that it jabbed me in the gut. All the ducks were lining up in perfect order.

"My spirit doesn't need any lifting," I finally answered him. "I'm feeling great again boys."

"Great!?" my friends questioned in unison.

"Grand."

"Grand?" they countered with amazement.

"Stupendous," I swaggered, upping the level of my fine temper.

"But how?" Craig queried.

"Acceptance, my best friend. I'm thirty-five. To a music executive I may as well be Benny...Goodman. I'm finished...I'm done. It happens a ton."

"I call it 'hell no, there's more you're not telling me,'" Craig challenged.

"And I call it bull...pucky," Link chortled.

Both Link and Craig stared silently at me, waiting for a more reasonable explanation for my dramatically altered and upbeat outlook.

"All right, all right," I conceded. "A few days ago, I was down, all right, real low, okay?"

"We saw that," Craig smirked.

"Sure. But then it hit me. All my dreams, the wishes I hid in my heart, they haven't been for me, guys. I've been dreaming..." I took out my wallet and flipped it open to show a picture of Jewel and my children to the boys. "I've been dreaming for them. And I can still make my dreams come true."

"I'm listening. I'm listening," Craig said excitedly.

"It's not even going to be hard. Jewel's a hell of a catch, right?"

Link and Craig looked skyward, then glanced at each other before answering as one voice. "Oh, Lord, you know she is." They both seemed carried away with zeal. "She's got that…"

"Right—she just hasn't been caught by the right guy. And I know thousands of men with diamond hooks are out there dying to pull her in. I've just gotta step out of the way and let 'em."

"So you're gonna leave her?" Craig asked with disbelief in his voice.

"Oh, no sir. She's gonna leave me."

Both of my friends' minds were churning with bewilderment. "How?" they asked. But before I even had a chance to answer, Link scolded me with more from the newfound adult in him. "I don't care how. That's ridiculous."

"She loves you too much," Craig interjected. "That's nuts. That's stupid!"

"You'll see. I'll drive her away. Then she'll do better than me in no time," I corrected him, revealing what I didn't know at the time was only the skeletal outline of my guaranteed plan. "I'll do what I have to do…anything. There's no fear when you know you're acting with honor."

"Benny, you're my friend, my best friend, so it's hard

for me to tell you this...but I think you're going insane." Craig shook his head, still dumbfounded by what he was hearing.

"Craig, I gotta do this. I have to make up...to make a real sacrifice, for everything I've put them through. Okay? I've got to," I drilled back.

"Your heart is in the right place, buddy...your mind's nowhere near that right place."

"I have to try, Craig; I have to. And you have to trust me. I mean, look at me," I instructed with a jubilant smile. "I couldn't be happier already."

The truth is I couldn't have been happier. Jewel was my high school sweetheart. She adored me and placed trust in me. Hell, Craig and Link weren't joking. My wife was a find. She could have had any guy she wanted, anytime she wanted. But she had faith in my talent and ability.

Why? I sold her on it, that's why. I thought that I was hot. I knew how to write music. Lyrics dropped from my lips like gold drivel, and I could vocalize them like a magician. The nerve I had, calling myself, *Magic*. But I believed I was a sure-thing winner as an artist.

It's not that I was lazy. I worked my job for bread and used what time I had left to develop my talent. All along I was right...there, as the great Garland would gesture. I was absolutely convinced I was on the verge—a thousand times. What I didn't know was that the hair width of a distance between here and there is an eternity in destiny's mercurial voyage. I was a stupid kid, a boy living in an imaginary enchanted land. I was even worse than that. I had seduced this gorgeous human being into my delusion.

I owed her; in my mind it was that simple. That's what the score was that night when I told Link and Craig my plan. I was going to force her to shove me out of her life, just like Jimbo had mentioned his wife did to him. I was confident that then at last after she met the right man, she and the children would be taken care of properly. Why wouldn't I be overjoyed?

My conviction was further reinforced by those same words uttered by the dying man, and the similar proclamation from Link. I was doing what was right—the noble, honorable thing—and it was going to be "the best thing for everyone." If I had to die accomplishing my purpose, then that would be the cost of setting things straight. I'd had my chance to measure up and came in short by an embarrassing too many lengths. The children were young enough that they could still have the opportunities I'd failed to provide for them. There are times when we have to step aside and do the manly thing.

I know most anyone would have been inclined to call me a stupid fool. But the fact is it didn't seem at all folly to me at the time. Truthfully, I still believe that what I did, as extreme as it would be in the end, wouldn't have seemed for many people that poorly conceived. It made sense, but in all fairness, probably nobody would have thought to do it but me. Hell, that's what makes what I did, and what happened after I did it, so extraordinary.

All this bold talk and expression of elevated spirits, however, was not without the offsetting feelings of sorrow I carried with me while I worked to spin out my plan. As insistent as I was to stuff my less-jubilant emotions below the threshold of perception, I do know that during this phase of what I'll deem my "fiasco," there were moments when I'd notice a powerful urge to break down in tears. That day at Jimbo's, in front of Craig and Link, I refrained from even exhibiting a dewy eye, let alone a meltdown. My emotions may have been jumbled, but the comfort of resolution was all I would permit publicly; that is until a couple of days later.

*****

Breaking down Jewel so she'd boot me out, took discipline and conviction; it also presented an unanticipated consequence: making myself scarce at home resulted in me having an abundance of free time on my hands. Thus, after work I'd frequently stop off at a small coffee shop not too far from home. I'd talk nonsense occasionally with another lonely soul or read the paper. Generally, I believe I was acquainting myself with what the rest of the world had been up to while I had been spending my life toiling at work or at home engaged in family matters or practicing my craft. It awed me that people passed their leisure time sipping a coffee or tea and playing on their computers, iPads or iPhones any time of day.

The place I went to most frequently was called Arnie's Coffee Bean and Tea Leaf. The owner named it after a more famous chain of stores, but it was a joke. He only had the one joint. He managed to tackle the big biz competition the old-fashioned way—he undercut the prices of the behemoths by so much that he had a thriving business.

I was nursing a cup of tea and browsing the paper, deliberating about how one single city could compete with the U. S. Government in its level of corruption. Police chief, city council members, building department, road and street maintenance—fraud charges smeared the columns of the local paper with the stench of a slaughterhouse.

There was a man sitting next to me. I'd noticed him several times in the past, but we'd never shared more than a glancing acknowledgment. He was my senior by well over two decades; his crewed bright grey hair indicated to me that he might have flipped off sixty a few years past. When he stood, I noticed he was a short man, six inches under my six-foot frame. He appeared well conditioned and on the slender side.

Most outstanding was that in spite of his age, he exuded youthfulness, more aptly, childishness. What fascinated me was how his physical movements were boyish; he stepped with vigor and had a rhythmic, light, free, stride, as if he were dancing. His face was thin, and when he smiled, which he seemed fond of doing, his cheeks popped forward, causing the formation of two ravines that descended from the bridge of his nose, dissolving into the corners of his lips. Otherwise, his skin was baby smooth, reinforcing the impression of a man years younger than his actual age.

Along the lines of my prior admission to moments of sadness, I'll further disclose that around this time, I sometimes had a real crying jag, and for no apparent reason. The most distressing part of this was that initially these instances came on with no warning. Out of fright of being exposed publicly, when I became adept at sensing the onset of one of these potentially embarrassing experiences, I'd seek refuge from humiliation by staying away from people. I developed such an effective way of concealing these intrusive sensations that not a soul on earth knew of them. I had become so clever at managing the feelings that they sometimes played hide and seek with me. I wasn't used to those types of emotions and can't say that I was thrilled when I encountered the stronger side of such affect.

This particular afternoon at Arnie's, when by chance I found myself sitting beside the stranger, I noticed that he was reading a book. The title had something to do with the differences between males' and females' personalities. He might have noticed me staring because he turned my way and addressed me.

"For some time now, I've been on a journey trying to understand my feelings better," he shared with a smirk. "My girlfriend kept telling me I was closed off. I didn't know what she was talking about. But since this was the first time in my entire life I'd found love in a relationship, I permitted her to convince me to explore what she way trying to explain. That's the motive for all the reading I've been doing."

"Maybe I should get a copy of that book," I responded half-jokingly. "I'm surprised myself by how far down I can go."

"You'll never surprise me when it comes to suffering. I've discovered that she was right. I've had a few crises in my life and never addressed them. During the past several months I've shed enough tears to fill a lady's wish. Recently, I even granted myself a certificate in despondency," he disclosed. "How's that for an honor?"

He didn't dismiss his pronouncement with a smile or comical gesture. He was shameless.

Normally, his statement might have repulsed me, but curiously I felt drawn to him. Looking back, I believe it was his overall demeanor; the tonal quality of his voice as he spoke, that especially is what hooked me. His expressions conveyed compassion and empathy, such that the words he uttered seemed subordinate to the feeling behind them. Hearing him reminded me of a lullaby, something that I'd never experienced from a male.

"I have to admit I've had some experience with

moping myself," I confessed to the stranger; my impulse to run and hide heightened as I noticed my eyes starting to moisten.

"Well, you're looking at a pro-caliber guy. Ask my lady about weeping if you want," he generously offered. I believe he wanted to lighten the weight of my burden. "Don't you worry; we'll find an answer to what's ailing you."

I preferred trying to veer toward the lighter side, dodging entirely what he was referring to. Yet, shockingly, I had no impulse to run, something I would have done under different circumstances. "I didn't know I was going to get psychotherapy thrown in for free along with my tea today."

"Just a little empathy for a fellow traveler who's bumping up against his female personality."

"Wait a second," I said as I wiped my eyes with the back of my hand. I laughed awkwardly before continuing, "This is embarrassing enough, and then to make it worse, you're calling me a lady?"

"Get with it pal," he said in a comically patronizing manner. "The man who doesn't acquaint himself with the female side of his character is a cripple. And by the way, I'm Simon." He introduced himself not only by extending his hand to shake but using his free limb to pat me gently on the shoulder.

"I'm Benny," I responded as we clasped hands. He then

reclined backward in a slumped posture, shooting out his short legs like probes searching for unpopulated land.

"I guess you'd conclude that I was crippled from not being able to get out my emotions before all this happened." I stopped to contemplate a topic clearly foreign to me. "All this weeping is my female side? Bringing it to the surface, does that mean I'll heal?" I mocked.

"Heal? Now then, for that you'd have had to have a disease or illness."

"Well, I've certainly not been my normal healthy self lately," I disclosed.

"That's when the female tendency in a man is most critical. You see, trying to keep all the feeling and hurt undercover, that's the man all right, the strong warrior. But without tempering that masculine strength with gentleness, sensitivity, and compassion, a man becomes dangerously hardened."

"Simon, this is all new to me."

"It might be. But what I'm sharing with you can prove invaluable to what's causing hurt for you…"

"Well, it's a bit of a complicated period in my life; you got me there. But life isn't supposed to be without challenge, is it Simon?"

"Mine never has been. But remember, whatever is eating at you, don't shut down what you're feeling because that's where your inner strength will come from."

"The lady will grant me power, right?"

"Exactly."

"I don't suppose you'd like to talk about the Tigers' game?" I intentionally employed humor to ease my discomfort.

"Sure, if you can stop whimpering like a lady," he dug at me for fun.

I shook my head in disbelief. Simon was a different animal than I was used to. Heck, I believe he had unexpectedly evolved into a different animal than he was used to.

I'd meet him many times after our initial encounter. At first, we'd randomly appear at the same time at the same shop. Then, as time passed, we became accustomed to each other's schedules, and the visits were silently planned and more frequent. As it turned out, my analysis was not over. In fact, during one of our early chance encounters, I reiterated to him how distressing it was struggling through as tough an experience as I was facing. He asked me a slug of questions and was genuinely interested in my circumstances. In fact, he went so far as to pry unabashedly for details, though I now realize that at that time I dodged around discussing my perfect plan or my marriage.

"By the questions you're asking, it appears you want to get to know me from the beginning," I commented. I was just getting acquainted with him but was sure by that time that he would have gladly spent the whole day digesting my history like one of his pop psychology books.

"Yes," he assured me. "Actually from when you were born."

"Yeah, right," I said dismissively.

"No. I'm not joking."

"This is about what is happening in real time, Simon."

"I know. But how you handle the situation might be connected in some way with your past, right? So, as the issues come up, you might get to places where you are blocked inside, where you feel stuck. That would suggest you're butting up against historical obstacles—some argue that these hurts are left over ego-damage from prior lives…but that's another discussion."

"I don't know about that but the historical idea, it's possible…I guess." I nodded, complimenting him on what I thought a brilliant insight. "Simon, the psychologist. Cool."

"Actually, I'm experimenting with being a writer," he chuckled. "You may be my next story. But let me give you a tip for your project, an artist who is not a psychoanalyst might as well be an undertaker."

"I'm not a writer and have no intention of trying."

"I understand. But you're taking a bruising, I can tell."

"I wouldn't go that far. It's painful, I'll admit. But I have a plan that's going to straighten things out real nice. The sun is peeking out already. Gradually, I'm making progress. For the most part, I'm feeling inspired about my life; after all, I'm the one willing what I'm going through."

"I'll be here to listen to you, eager to see how all this pans out."

"Like I told you, Simon, I have a perfect plan. It has to work out great," still withholding details.

He looked at me without expression. Years of experience might have taught him more about "perfect plans" than I understood at the time.

I left Simon that afternoon. When I did, I was aware that I was still bothered by a lingering thought from our first meeting—a little lady persona worming around in the soul of Benny Wright? Earlier, I had clobbered the foreign contaminant but now recognized that until I addressed the idea, it would rise up to stick its tongue out at me any time it wished.

There was another issue gnawing at my mind. I had told Craig and Link that there was going to be a white knight riding in atop a handsome stallion, bringing wealth and opportunity to Jewel and the children. Who that might be I had no idea. Worse, I hadn't even considered the simple matters of how or when.

Logic was not part of my plan; when a man is in the kind of pain I was in, he believes he's acting rationally, but the truth is he's driven by raw emotions, as caustic as pure hot peppers. Who was it going to be that would fill the void I left in my family, and when would it happen?

Now, those are dumb questions.

CHAPTER 8: DISSOLVING BONDS

It was several days after talking with Simon about the female side of the male personality that I next ran into him at our haunt. He seemed his normal relaxed self, sipping on a tea and picking at a bagel. He ordered it plain and pulled tiny pieces of it with his fingers; it lasted for hours.

He always dressed casually. From what I could tell, his wardrobe was not going to build credit card debt. He faithfully wore faded blue jeans and t-shirts of various colors, but all with an insignia that I didn't recognize. I noticed, like a pack of cigarettes, he kept a small box filled with jellybeans rolled up in the sleeve of his shirts. Every so often he'd reward himself with one of his sweets, and when he did he'd never fail to offer me as many as I cared to take. I thought the candy had to be a reformed cigarette habit. He had a sole distinguishing physical characteristic, a tattoo; a tiny grey dolphin on the fleshy part of his right forearm, just above the wrist.

"I've been thinking about this female inside the man business," I sheepishly began.

"I'm glad to hear that. It's not that bad, is it?"

"I don't know yet."

"Well, Benny, I promise it's no crime getting in touch with a sensitive and tender part of your personality; that's all I'm trying to tell you."

"It would probably be better to say that those parts of myself are getting in touch with me rather than me with them; bashing me might even be a better way to describe it."

"It's good for you," Simon elated. "Lots of men repress it entirely, and that's why they're often a bit grim on the surface."

"Well, you're not glum, for sure. But I'll level with you, Simon, I sense quite a bit of fierceness in you, you know that?"

"Sure. I'm a tough nut. Like I said, I've lived through trauma."

"Like what?" I impulsively asked, not considering that I might be overstepping the bounds of propriety.

"Look up Marine Special Forces operations on the Internet. Then tell me what you find," he chortled, after which he paused long enough to send a message. "I'll save you the trouble. Nothing. The Special Forces exist but nobody knows or is supposed to know what they really do. I can't tell you what I did, but I can show you what my reward was for four years of service."

The shop was near empty and we were sitting alone in a corner. Simon lifted his white t-shirt and turned for me to view his backside. He looked like a tic-tac-toe game, with deep, ugly crevices of scar tissue running diagonally, horizontally, and vertically. I could hardly stand a glance.

"Anyone who went through what I did and lived has to be tough. What I realized came long after the fact. For years, I blasted my way through and past the emotions that were soldered to the tormented memories I hauled home with me from the war. Busted marriages and affairs, broken families, night sweats, and drunken' brawls; I fought like a soldier more after my discharge than during my service.

"You wouldn't have witnessed me shedding a tear or expressing doubt or insecurity. Then I met Patty," he smiled hugely, "and that's when I learned the wonder of a good sob. The whole experience, however—hurting and healing, healing and hurting, alternately, over and over—is what caused me to appreciate what I never would have, had I not drawn from an archaic well in my psyche something that I associated more with what I know to be female characteristics than male."

"Like what?"

"Permission to feel…permission to express my emotions. It's as simple as that. The more I had to let loose what I was feeling inside, the stronger I became. I thank my lady for the grit and love to stick with me. We're together, glued for whatever chapters of this life we have left."

"That's nice, Simon."

While complimenting him I was struck by a less comforting thought. Simon might be like a drug that was contraindicated for my condition. He's bonded to his lady because he opened the depths of his being to her, whereas I'm lifting anchor and sailing away from my woman because I can't share my torment. He was a fortunate man. I was a tragedy. I would have traded places with him in a wink.

The sad truth was that I had a mission to carry out that was absolutely necessary and correct. He couldn't understand, but the less "in touch" I was, the better. I dismissed Simon for the moment by concluding that emotions in a duel with reason will bulls-eye a bullet into the power of thought while the mind is still deliberating which handgun to use in its defense.

"At first, I thought that all the crying, self-pity, and dependence I had been displaying was weakening me, but she was right, it was exactly the opposite." He hesitated and then offered me a warning. "Much of the time, and with many people, I don't let those parts of my being come out; it's not wise under all conditions to show your full self."

"So I can relax that you're not going to show up here one of these times with a dress on?" I pocked at him.

"I promise."

"Well, in fairness, this female personality thing has to be my issue since I'm the one who brought it up."

"I don't really see it as an issue for you. Your awkwardness with it I understand. Most people don't accept it. Many women even cringe when tender emotions come from a man. Did you know that?"

"Not really, but while we're on the topic, what about women? Am I to presume they're harboring a macho man in their personality?"

"Makes sense to me. Women who make friends with the male in their psyche are strong and confident, surprisingly less defensive with men and able to be more loving. I think it's just plain common sense, Benny. That's how it came to me, living through it and then paying attention to what I was experiencing."

"Yeah. My wife's definitely got some man in her," I announced.

"That's good for her...and good for you. A woman who snivels and whimpers, who is meek and weak, always subservient and submissive, is going to elicit guilt from her male partners," he theorized.

"Come to think of it, I know what you're talking about. Jewel is becoming fiercely angry."

"Better to fight—keeps you from being alone."

"Sometimes we have no choice but to be alone, even when we have people we love."

"Oh, I know that one, Benny," Simon laughed. "Been there."

"Someday I'll tell you the whole story. I don't think you'll say you've been there after that."

"I apologize. I don't mean to take anything away from your suffering."

"If only you could."

"You wouldn't let me anyway, Benny. You'll have to play this out on your own. I can tell that. But I'll be here for you; that you can count on."

"Then I'll have someone to fight with."

"True, unless you bail. You see, Benny, a deep relationship is in part about fighting. When you quarrel, you slam up against another human force, you touch and feel them. I don't believe any person senses aloneness when that happens. It's what we're all looking for, something real. The problem is that as the encounters become more and more human, we become afraid and look for the closest emergency exit."

"Damn, you must have been a hit in the Marines, Simon."

"Funny. I never used to be like this; I never used to think."

During this period, I found myself less and less looking forward to seeing Simon. I actually often contemplated avoiding him. He was drawing me deeper into my being. It was like gravity. I couldn't feel it but it embraced me in its force, holding me helplessly like a letter in a word. All I could consciously experience was the thought that this man was threatening to me, to my plan. In spite of this, I couldn't resist visiting Arnie's at precisely the times I knew I'd bump into him.

*****

After I had disclosed my plan to Craig and Link at Jimbo's, I kept up the pressure on Jewel. Every night I stayed out. I ignored her angry outbursts and snubbed the pleas by my children that I stay home. I figured that the more force I put on all of them, the sooner she'd get the picture and send me packing.

That's not how it worked.

I had to go a step further than what I'd envisioned initially in my guaranteed plan—a key element needed to be added. I had been premature in calling my approach "perfect."

I remember that it was a Saturday morning when things started to heat up. I came into the living room. Dion must have been waiting for me. He was at his desk wearing headphones, with his guitar and keyboard out.

Dion is sort of the opposite of his sister. He's a quiet, reserved, and somewhat introverted kid. He's moody like we would have expected his pre-adolescent sister to be, but then again, he was eerily similar in temperament to my pop. What distinguished him from my father, and what really elevated the boy's spirit, was music—poor kid, he'd inherited a bad trait from his old man.

That morning, when I came in, he looked up at me. I could tell he had something he wanted to share, but as I'd been doing day in and day out, I moved to the front door to exit before he had a chance to catch me. I must have moved too slow or he was unusually fast in intercepting me.

"Dad, you gotta hear this," he shouted over the sound he had an instant before started to play at the keyboard.

"I've gotta go, son."

"It'll only take a minute," he whined.

"Sorry, busy day," I responded impatiently, and with a note of intolerance.

"It's Saturday," Dion reminded me.

"I know it is, but I've got a meeting."

"It's been like this for weeks."

"Too busy, that's all!"

I started for the door. I was about to pull on the handle when I heard his more urgent appeal.

"Please! Just listen to this one. I've been working on it for days. It's the song I'm doing next week for a concert at school."

"Okay, just for a minute," I said, as if I was making a grand concession.

"Fine," he rifled back at me with mixed satisfaction and irritation.

I knew I was tearing the kid up, getting him more

riled with me by the minute. At the same time, I sensed his desperation to get a piece of my attention, to reclaim the dad he'd always had. He had no idea how it pained me to hold myself away from him, from all of them. Still, I felt compelled to deliver the message to the whole family that it was time for them to move on. Determined to drive home that point is what propelled me to gallop to the door and get out. It was the only sane thing to do since I had resolved that there was no turning back. By then I knew, contrary to Simon's prescription, that the only way to succeed was to harden my feelings.

What he had created on his own was remarkable for a boy his age. It doubly bothered me that I couldn't let on how much I appreciated and admired his work. He titled his song, "My Fantasy Life." I can recite many of his lyrics off the top of my head.

> *It's time to climb and be, at the top of the world I'm dyin' to see, my fans in my hand with a mic, so I can get livin' my fantasy life. I got a whole lotta livin' to go, and I ain't plannin' on livin' like an average Joe. I know I got the tools to get to the top of the times and make the rules.*

> *Well, I want what I want and I got what I need to reach it, I know just what to flaunt so I leave y'all sittin' speechless. It's a simple phenomenon, ain't nobody like me, I'm far beyond. Soon I'll be commandant, with the world in the grip of my palm.*

My pop used to always say that if you get
good you're bound to make way. Well, I got
some sweet tricks and soft tone, a million lines
and a style of my own.

While Dion was repeating the chorus for the fourth time, Shana heard the music and came bounding into the room, adding to the performance an impromptu dance choreographed to the beat. When Dion finished displaying his work, I was more determined than ever to get the "H" out of the house. I tried to dismiss him quickly.

"Great. Great, Dion," I said with indifference. "I gotta go."

"Wait!" Dion implored. "'Gotta go' is all I hear from you anymore. I tell you 'bout a track I wrote, and you say…"

Jewel heard the commotion and had come into the room. Shana was already there, and the three joined together at precisely the same moment to say, "Gotta go?"

"I show you my new jazz tap steps," Shana scoffed—executing on the spot for my enjoyment a couple quick moves—"you say…"

"Gotta go," the three harmonized.

"I say I miss a man that can make me smile," Jewel said sadly, "you say…"

All three repeated together, "Gotta go."

Dion wasn't finished with me. Jewel and Shana were not either.

105

"Why do we keep fightin' for your time, Pop?" Dion rifled.

"Why do we keep battlin' for a tiny little drop?" Shana rhymed her question. "You used to wanna see me dance atop my toes, so why do you keep actin' like you've found a better show? "

"You used to always joke around with me 'til you got a laugh. Now when I look at you, it's always your back half," Jewel added mournfully.

"No matter what we show you, you say gotta go!" they shouted in unison.

That was it for me. Talk about feeling. It was more than I could handle and we weren't finished.

"We're right here, waiting," Jewel whispered within earshot of the children, while at the same time sidling up to me.

I stood mute, still impatient to leave. She kept staring at me, imploring me to open up, but I resisted.

"Benny, I know it can't be," she stammered, "but I've got to ask." I could see her raising an imaginary banner with a dreaded question printed on it. Her tone of voice spelled a subtle threat. "There isn't another woman, is there?"

On the soul of my children, I had never thought of that. By now it had been weeks of me intentionally rejecting them and behaving heedlessly, yet not making a measure of progress on my plan. I was getting sick of sucking up the guilt I was manufacturing by the bucket-ful—impatient to get things moving.

Then, when she asked me about another woman, I reflectively cocked my head because I realized sub-consciously that her comment had tweaked a critical thought. *Fool,* I thought to myself. *There's only one thing that's going to convince this woman I'm flowing out of her life. I need a good old-fashioned hot fling.*

The one thing my lady would not tolerate was another woman. I was dead certain of it. That was the first time the word "die" from the murdered man's last statement made sense to me. The relationship had to die, and I was about to take out an axe and hatchet it to breathlessness. I needed to convince my wife that my balls were made of steel.

"A what?" I responded to Jewel's query.

"Another woman," she snapped back at me.

I hesitated before responding to her. My mind was working on a vague notion, and I was trying to filter out distractions. But then by chance my phone went off. When I looked at the screen, I noticed that it was Garland. I glanced at Jewel, leaving her with no reply. Instead, I answered the call.

"Hey, Garland."

"That was a question, Benny," Jewel forcefully inter-jected in a not-too-kindly manner.

"Just give me a minute," I sharply replied to my wife.

"Sup, Garland…I know you love me, but I told you I'm out of the biz."

I listened to him talk. I couldn't believe what I was hearing. It was all coming together, as if Jewel and Garland were unwittingly acting to bring me good fortune. I let Garland rattle on with his message as I began to formulate what I was going to do to get things moving with Jewel.

"Great opportunity to be exposed, huh? Everyone's going to be there," I muttered while digesting the remainder of what I knew for certain was an offer motivated by anything other than regard for my career. "Alright. Put me on the list."

I flashed fiendish white teeth in Jewel's face. I could tell it irked her. She was standing strong and impatient, tapping her right foot on the floor like a mean twitch. It seemed an eternity that we stood staring at one another. I refused to let my eyes tell her how much I wanted to cry. She held her ground. Her inquisitive glare was unyielding. Finally, I broke the silence.

"Sorry, Jewel. No. Okay?" I answered with a casualness that had to sting. "I'm late; I've…" I intentionally paused to mimic her and the children. "Gotta go."

Jewel never relinquished her eye contact. Her face was blank, as if she were processing the fact that she had to believe me because it was I, Benny Wright, who had said the word—the only one she could imagine hearing—"no." Yet an inner conflict she must have never imagined she'd experience was raging. She couldn't trust what I was saying because Benny Wright, her love, had disembarked from port and was drifting further and further away from shore.

I had told her the truth. The cause for her doubt was not grounded in reality but rather in instinct. She knew at that point I was capable of the worst, of destroying forever the love we shared.

So while affairs, and their possible consequence to a matrimonial bond, will become a plot in this adventure, it should not be mistaken as the overarching theme. For what drives my story is desperation, with infidelity merely throwing a tantrum. This tale depicts what actions that wretched state of despondency can drive a man to perform. It paints a sad but true picture of the extent to which a man will go to try and overcome the beating hopelessness can deliver.

CHAPTER 9: MEETING MISS COOKIE

I had planned to spend that Saturday afternoon with a couple of guys from work, taking in a ballgame. But after the intriguing call from Garland, while Jewel was confronting me about an affair, I cancelled going out with my colleagues—there was work to be done now that my little plan was being modified into something closer to perfection. As soon as I was out the door that morning, I grabbed my cell. It might have been the most momentous call that I'd ever made. In fact, an hour later, I was due at Jimbo's to meet up with a friend. I had no idea that my best buddy, Craig, along with Link, would be there. I was all the more pleased that they were, taking their presence as a sign foreshadowing the success of the implementation of the next stage of my program.

It was a particularly clear spring day, the sunlight

brightening Jimbo's in a frightful manner. The light shone so strong it was close to sending away customers. Those present were struggling to see past the glare on several of the TV screens hanging on the walls and just above the bar. Jimbo hated closing the blinds but would have no choice if clouds didn't land soon.

Before I arrived, Link and Craig had taken seats at a table and were soothing the wounds left from a week of shifts at the factory with a pitcher of Budweiser beer.

"To the best place in the city to spend the day," Link cheered as he raised his glass to tap Craig's.

"I hear it'll be seventy degrees out today, and sunny," Craig celebrated.

"Well, it is seventy degrees out today right in here. And I won't get burnt either."

"That's why I love you all," Jimbo crowed from behind the bar. "Who could ask for a better customer than a drunk? There couldn't be a more loyal breed in the wor…"

His clowning with the regulars was interrupted. A lone female entered. She flicked her head, commanding her long black hair to settle over her left shoulder. The movement of the shampoo commercial quality strands was of such prestige that the patrons had to steady their hearts by swallowing deep breaths of air.

"Hi, fellows," she flirtatiously greeted the boys.

She headed straight for the bar and took a seat.

111

"Can I help you, dear?" Jimbo asked as if he were a predator offering a sweet to a child.

"Not yet. I think I'll just take a peek at the ballgame."

She tilted her neck backward so she could stare at the screen above her. She was an avid Tiger fan and today the home team was taking on the Yankees in enemy territory, New York.

It was still early in the season, but every game was a nail biter to her. The team was playing on enemy turf and she'd arrived just in time for the opening ceremony; it was half past one. Still, that was not the purpose of her unprecedented visit to the esteemed world of Jimbo's.

While awaiting the person she had come to see, she used the free time to check out a few pitches. She was excited because her favorite player, Justin Verlander, was on the mound.

She knew it was a silly infatuation, falling for a pro star pitcher. Still, he was damn cute in her opinion. She'd invented her own fantasies about the "kind and gentle man." His hair was always under his cap, but he sported a thick beard of dark brown and he kept it finely trimmed. She loved especially that several strands twisted in the center of his chin, creating the effect of a tiny dimple. His teeth were large—likely orthodontic straightened—and clear white, and along with his horizontally elongated eyes that to her glittered, he seemed always animated and jolly.

She had watched him enough times, however, to

know that there was another side to him. When he was called to work for the next inning, he'd gruffly pull off his black-hooded Tiger sweatshirt and toss it like a warrior on the bench. Then, on the plate, pitching for her beloved team, he was fierce. He'd stare menacingly at the opposing batter. With some of them, he'd take an especially long pause between pitches, chewing on either a piece of gum or tobacco, making sure the hitter could feel his heat.

She'd admit it—but only to her best friend—that watching Verlander made her body hot and wet, a feeling only one other man she knew had given her, a secret that up to then she'd never disclosed to another being; that man was me, Benny Wright. Why these two completely different types of males caused her feelings to be overpowered, she couldn't explain. As for Justin Verlander, it was pure imagination, for she had never met the man. A few times she had gone out to Comerica Park to watch him pitch, but the bleachers were as close as she'd come to connecting with her idol. She wondered…if by chance she could pass by as he was leaving the park, would he take an interest.

Cookie Acosta was a knockout and she knew it. Bringing a man to true religion took no more for her than snuggling her fine frame into a pair of jeans by that very name. True Religion began with a photo shoot of a girl trying to look as sexy as Cookie Acosta, giving it her all to work her way into a man's libidinal soul by swishing and swaying her derriere down the boulevards of any city—no one could do it like Cookie.

Truth was, owing to my love for Jewel, she had been able to attract the same level of non-attention from yours truly as she had from Justin Verlander, and that was in spite of the fact she had known me for several years. She had even worked directly with me on many occasions. She wondered if she was no more than a foolish child who always managed to place her amorous wishes where they were sure to be dashed, while the universe of available men was thirsting to satisfy her every whim and fancy.

Her presence at Jimbo's was an event that quickly sent the stock value of the Detroit Tigers plunging. From the moment she had walked in the door, she was the only person in the establishment watching the game.

"May I ask what brings you to Jimbo's?" the owner simpered, while sneaking in a glance at one of the most luscious ladies he'd ever set eyes on.

"Sure. I'm meeting a man named Benny."

Before a conversation could be initiated between Cookie and Jimbo, both Craig and Link were on their way to the bar to see if they might impress the lady. Hearing the opportunity, they each made their pitch.

"I'm Benny," Link said as he rushed over to her seat.

"No, I'm Benny," Craig corrected his friend.

Cookie was giggling by the antics being played out in her honor. "Nice try, boys. But I know Benny."

Meeting Miss Cookie

She was not just a sexy and beautiful lady. She was a shockingly sexy and beautiful woman. She had shown no mercy preparing for her meeting at Jimbo's—she had come for business and dressed accordingly.

The cut of a pair of jeans, the fit of a top as it hugs the curves and lines of a woman's figure, the mystery of painted eyes, the flow and glow of meticulously combed hair, and the authority of a pair of bright red leather, high-heel shoes all are tools a woman can use to arouse interest in the opposite sex. Cookie could do all that with little effort. But what elevated her to a plane where few of the female order stood, was a sixth dimension, a factor only a select group of women could conceive, let alone equal. She was pure and simple griddle hot at the most elemental cellular level, and there was little she could have done had she tried to conceal it.

With Link and Craig hustling in the vicinity of Cookie, neither noticed when I waltzed in the door. I walked over to where Cookie was seated. I offered a high-five to my friends and then greeted Cookie with a hug.

"Cookie, good to see you...and welcome to my home away from home. Allow me to introduce you to Jimbo's regulars," I offered magnanimously.

"Pleasure is all mine," Cookie sung out with a wink at all of the men.

I guided Cookie by the arm and was about to lead her to a table at the corner of the bar.

"Benny, I'm...gonna be going." There was

115

unmistakable discomfort and confusion in Craig's voice, no doubt due to seeing me with Cookie. "Seventy degrees and sunny is sounding too good to pass up," he proclaimed as he intercepted us before we could sit.

"I'll be taking off with you, pal," Link eagerly signed on.

The two left. I proceeded with Cookie to a table.

"I thought you forgot about me," Cookie began.

"No one could forget you, Cookie." I flattered the woman seeming to have no shortage of attention even after the exit of my friends.

"You'd be surprised how easily I've been forgotten. Cookie, nothing but a pretty surface and," she stopped to display her figure, "they all assume there's nothing deeper."

"Today I need the surface...but someday I may want more of what's underneath."

"Benny, if you're ever ready to take a look at the true me you'll be the first to cash in."

"And I'll keep that redeemable coupon where I can get it quickly," I pledged to her with an assuring smile, patting my wallet as I imitated placing an imaginary card inside for safekeeping.

I would have never conceived it at the time but what she was referring to as hidden "underneath" was going to play a key role in my life.

"Okay, but what does that mean today, Benny? You need a backup singer?"

"No, not backup this time," I answered with a slow sideways movement of my head, enough to convey negation and at the same time elicit intrigue.

"Then, Benny, you may for the first time be singing my tune," Cookie elated melodiously.

Cookie had worked with me many times in the past, doing vocals on tracks I had recorded and backing me up at local gigs. Still, I'd never taken the time to get to know much about her personal life. Through her involvement in this affair, I came to know her far more intimately.

As our relationship developed, she disclosed that she found me to be an even-tempered and soothing man. She envisioned me entirely different from most of the males she'd been associated with in her life. With what I had in mind, I wasn't sure she'd hold that same complimentary view of me for long.

Part of her opening up included an accounting of her early history. Cookie had been abused. During her upbringing, her violent father beat her numerous times. In between the belt and knuckle lessons, he was intimidating to the point she knew nothing but terror in his presence. Then, to make her home environment even worse, her father took pleasure in ignoring the mistreatment of Cookie's sadistic older brother who delighted in sexually tormenting her…something he did repeatedly until one day when at age fifteen she stabbed him with a screwdriver she'd intentionally placed next to her bed.

117

She left home later that day and never returned. From then on, she walked the earth as if she owned the men that dwelled there. Her ability to arouse their appetite for lust, along with an aloofness and indifference, made her all the more sought after. The obvious fact that her attractiveness was crafted with a measure of exoticness and eroticism only increased her worth to the men hoping they might get a shot.

During the time we spent together, she shared an unimaginable fact. Other than the forced sexual traumas with her brother, she was as inexperienced as a virgin. She longed to be loved but couldn't afford the risk of the beatings she was sure would come her way once she permitted herself to become dependent on a relationship.

Thus, the outward persona of ostentation and brazenness that she flaunted was a sham—prior to dating me, she was scared of intimacy and was willing to admit it. She also knew that somehow along the path of her horrid life, she had acquired the virtues of honor and integrity. She wanted to do something worthy for the world and saw no possible channel to accomplish it other than through expressing her passion in song.

When she examined the whole of her being—and she was a lady quite capable of reflection in private moments—she concluded that the only man she knew she could trust and who shared her high morals and values was me. Now, finally, her moment had arrived—I needed her. And it wasn't just to bust out a tune on a new beat I'd written. No, this time the man was hurting, and Cookie Acosta was an expert at licking wounds.

"I want to take you to a party this Saturday night, that's all," I giggled.

"A date? You want to take me out?"

"If you'd allow me."

Cookie had never met Jewel. Frankly, she knew nothing about my wife. She had never brought up the subject of my marriage prior to my placing the call to meet her at Jimbo's. But her imagination set to work after I approached her. Immediately, she contemplated the level of mistreatment the woman would have to be inflicting on her husband to get a man like me to violate the marital bond. She knew most men routinely had affairs, but not a man of the stature to which she had elevated me.

"Benny, I've always wondered about you," she responded with a thrilling tear forming in her eye.

"Have you?"

"Well, you've never made a pass, never thrown a line, never given a wink." Cookie shrugged her shoulders and smiled alluringly. "You know, some say that's a crime."

"Well, I'm no criminal," I laughed. "Listen, there's lots of music industry people coming to Garland's affair. It certainly won't hurt your career."

"You. Important people. Sounds irresistible."

"So you're in, Cookie?"

I took no precautions to keep my conversation with Cookie private. Obviously, to the contrary—I advertised it. One of the regulars sitting at a table next to us—one of the men who knew me—had been listening to us talk while downing shots of whisky. It was still the first inning of the game. When the interloping neighbor heard me appealing for Cookie's consent, he couldn't resist clowning in on our talk.

"And if you don't want to go with Benny, I'll take you, pretty thing," the man generously offered.

"I'll be sticking with Benny, but thanks anyways," Cookie gently rejected his drunken gesture.

Her short visit to Jimbo's had earned her a better reward than even Justin Verlander could have delivered, especially on this afternoon when Monsieur Star-Pitcher was getting roughed up early. She was eager to keep the gift I'd given her alive in her heart as long as she could—she stood up briskly.

"Bye, boys." She gleefully waved to her audience as she departed.

"Bye, bye," resounded a collection of voices from each corner of the joint.

"And Benny," Cookie smiled, "I'll think of something...unusual to wear."

"I bet you will," I laughed devilishly.

Cookie was good. Cookie wanted to do good things for the world. Cookie wanted to do good things for her new beau. If my wife was torturing me, was there a crime to be committed in allowing Cookie to soothe my hurt? It wasn't she who'd initiated inching in on another woman's territory—the man had come knocking on her door, and she was doing what any women in her circumstance would.

"Come in, baby. I'll make it all go away. Let Cookie love you back to health," she imagined saying to me as soon as I laid my bleeding heart in her arms.

This girl was a lethal weapon. She was at a minimum the type who might inspire violence in a wife facing infidelity. Did Benny Wright have a devious side to him, toying with a woman he knew in the end might be slain by his wife, in this case Jewel advancing the marital imperative with an ultimate and indisputable statement that the game was over?

CHAPTER 10: LET'S PARTY

Garland lived in the exclusive Grosse Pointe Farms area, his home facing Lake St. Clair. It was a Tudor style house with the structure dominated by a bold, grey-brick chimney that rose above the peak of the third story. Several acres of landscape surrounded the estate. There were expanses of green grass, but by far the most remarkable feature of the landscape was a collection of crimson King Norway maple trees scattered about the grounds.

It was nearing summer, and the trees had finished adorning their shaggy limbs with a full dressing of striking purple and green foliage. Cookie had never seen Garland's house and was overcome by the elegance and charm.

"Did we working class make a mistake? My, how does the man do it?" Cookie sighed.

There were several cars parked along the wide semi-circular driveway that ended close to the front entrance. Cookie and I exited my Chevy Sonic sedan and went to the front door. Cookie ran a couple steps ahead of me, making sure she was the first to ring the doorbell. Garland had seen my car pull up and came to greet us, clearly shocked to see me accompanied by a woman other than Jewel. He stood speechless for an instant before breaking into a wide grin as he inspected the bombshell of a lady with her left arm entangled in my right.

Cookie wasn't joking when she said she'd find something special to wear for the occasion. The evenings hadn't yet begun to warm up the way they would in a month, when summer would land in full force, so she had to be chilled in the outfit she'd designed.

*****

Describing how Cookie presented herself on our evening out at Garland's was one of the easier meetings I had with Simon—I saw him the day following the date with Cookie, and by that time my relationship with Simon was growing, even though I was resisting some of his influence with all my willpower.

Simon and I had been fingering through a stack of jellybeans that he'd poured onto a napkin, looking for our favorite flavors. Red-hot Cookie was the perfect topic as I took a bite of my cinnamon candy.

"She wasn't wearing much. It was hardly anything, if you get what I mean. Simon…stop looking at me so analytically," I giggled childishly.

"What are you talking about?" he responded.

"I'm telling you the universal sex goddess of mankind was standing next to me…and you know it; you're not that old."

"I'm not even old," he insisted.

"Fine. Then, what would you do if the most attractive lady you could imagine walked past you wearing the most revealing getup you've ever seen? You'd stand there without giving a glance, your heart wouldn't pump masses of blood to your groin, your throat wouldn't insist you swallow—even if you're right there with your lover?"

"I guess so, but I'm content with the lady I have."

"Damn, man. You introduced me to my inner lady. I guess I'll have to get you acquainted with your soul blood."

"I'm sure I have some."

"I hope so because what I'm getting at, Simon, is that to appreciate what I'm going to describe for you next, you might want to imagine being a brother."

"Okay. Let me put on my orange suit, a few pounds of gold necklaces and bracelets, and my two-karat diamond stud in my earlobe."

"You got it bro," I applauded—the man could be delightfully confounding. "Now, I'll get on with Miss

Cookie. She's wearing a black blouse made of some sort of thin lacy material. I don't know how she accomplished it, but you could see right through it to her breasts, but the top portion must have had a second piece of shear lining inside to prevent a full view of her nipples. The deep "V" cut in the top did nothing to conceal an inside shot of her anatomy—she wasn't at all huge, but what unmanned every male who saw her was that they stood firm and confident like rifled guards outside the doors of an embassy. Are you with me now, Simon? If not, I have more to arouse your interest."

"I knew all along I'd bring out the descriptive writer in you. Go ahead, Benny, but I may have to take a break and head home to visit my girlfriend, if you don't mind."

"That's it, my man. She'll be the happiest lady on earth and never know it was all courtesy of Cookie Acosta."

"So go on. You were saying about the two guards…"

"That's the beginning. The hair was the next treat. She cut it. I mean to say she sheared it. I noticed she kept running her fingers through the reddish-toned strands. I don't own such a vehicle, but I imagined that the reward of a hairdo like hers was how it could come out of a freeway ride in a convertible and not be pissed. Amazingly, on her it was as sexy as she'd intended it to be.

"Her lips were a bright red, matching the color she'd painted her finger- and toenails—she wanted blood that night and made no apologies for her greed. Her skirt was also black and it fitted skintight at a length that scantily covered her butt.

"When she walked, every inch of her body pulsed and thumped. It was just the way Cookie wanted it. It was the first time she had the man of her dreams with her, and she was making a statement that the queen had arrived and was not being dethroned."

"Your wife…"

"Jewel can hold her own just fine. But that night was all about Cookie."

"No, I mean what is Jewel going to say about this?"

"We'll get to that. Let me tell you about the rest of the party. It was quite the event."

*****

Garland was speechless looking at Cookie, which is saying something for him. I never realized he hadn't met her. While Cookie was previewing herself at the door, we both gazed inside, where numerous guests were sipping drinks and socializing. Finally, Garland recovered from the dual shocks of me without Jewel and my date's knockout appearance.

"Put you on the list, huh? You must have forgotten to mention your little 'plus one,'" Garland howled gleefully.

"Oh, you never met Cookie?" I asked him, delighted at his pause.

"It's my loss, I'm sure."

"Cookie sings backup for me from time to time." I

then turned to Cookie. "Cookie, this is my good friend and manager, Garland."

"Well, come on in," Garland suggested.

By now, the potential detonable device at my side was beginning to spread heat into the room. It was not only the men who inspected her, but more obvious was the effort on the part of the women to meander past the open front door to get a look at the competition.

"It's a pleasure to meet any good friend of Benny's," Cookie greeted Garland.

"Likewise, to a...good friend of Benny," Garland said to Cookie as he glanced curiously at me. Then, oddly, Garland dismissed himself. "Well, y'all have fun. I'm gonna go stir up some trouble of my own," he cackled before nearly sprinting across the room.

It's not easy to bring Garland to a state of awkwardness. He's the type of man who likes to keep life simple. I think he really didn't know how to handle not seeing Jewel with me. His solution was to duck the messiness. *Stir up some trouble of my own.* Garland was a card; one that a lucky man would not be dealt.

That evening at Garland's was to be the tipping point in my relationship with Jewel, and I had assigned Cookie the starring role in the drama. Had she not been so giddily infatuated with the good fortune to finally have a crack at the man she had fantasized being with, she might have discovered that she was acting in a production doomed from the get-go.

"Ready to impress?" Cookie asked me.

"I'm ready," I responded like a dive-bomber.

"What must all these people be thinking right now, seeing you without Jewel?" Cookie breezily posed to her date.

"Don't you worry yourself about it, not at all, darling."

Cookie stopped abruptly, transported from a dream state to what she calculated to be a first revelation.

"Hold on just a minute. Now it makes perfect sense," she said as she crept closer to me and gently patted my shoulder. "This all makes perfect sense. My poor man."

"You get what?" I asked her, now confused as to what she was concocting in her mind. "What all makes perfect sense now?"

"You want to be caught. I thought at first Jewel was abusing…mistreating you. But now I see it. Because you caught her cheating on you—that's worse." Then, she put her arms around me. "You poor man."

"I wish that were the case, Cookie. But this time, you're off track."

"Really!" Cookie declared more than asked.

"Really," I assured her.

"Damn, I guess I better be ready for it then."

"Ready for what?"

"Ready for Jewel. If I know women, and I think I do, things are gonna get…nasty, Benny. Women nasty. And that's the kind of nasty you gotta get ready for. Benny, it's the kind of nasty I wouldn't touch for anyone besides you."

"Jewel will be fine. You'll be fine too," I promised. "Now, just remember, Cookie, as we're talking with everyone this evening…"

"I'll be like fudge on a sundae," she promised, gesturing that she was prepared to play the role I'd rehearsed with her before we arrived at Garland's.

"A guy my age with a wife and two children is not artist material, unless he has a more…youthful outlook." I wiggled my body as I playfully poked Cookie in the rib.

"Okay, then. You think I'll do for a more youthful outlook?"

"Yeah, Cookie. It's you and me. We gotta take care of business, you know that."

"Are we gonna take care of business?" Cookie winked back provocatively.

"Let's mingle," I responded evasively.

It was about this time when Garland's secretary, Georgia, entered. She was holding a stack of papers and immediately disposed of them by placing the pile on a counter where she thought she'd direct Garland so he could sign them. She then waltzed directly to her boss. Addressing him, she held her right arm outstretched with the index finger ordered to point straight at the papers she wanted to bring to his attention. She rotated about forty-five degrees before the digit disobediently stopped. It had zeroed in on me, who now had my arm around the waist of Cookie Acosta. Georgia, a woman always in a state of animation and high-energy, was frozen in a long pose, her finger doggedly drawn toward the two of us like a sword.

"Holy shit!" is all she was able to utter.

By this point, Garland had recovered from the un-imagined circumstances of me not being with Jewel, as well as from Cookie's presence. He'd returned to his characteristic lightness. Softly, so that only Georgia—who was now standing next to him—could hear, he spoke to her. "Out with the old; in with the new. That's the name of the game."

Georgia couldn't begin to process what her eyes were beholding...nor her ears hearing. Jewel the old—this lush tramp the new? Another "Holy shit!" was all she could eke out.

The discomfort I was experiencing referred me back to a discussion I'd recently had with Simon. He was studying the human mind from varying cultural perspectives. What he came across was a body of knowledge suggesting that the ego portion of what we call the mind is entirely responsible for creating our reality, yet that very state is nothing but illusions.

In other words, we create the world at will, in our heads, as we choose, instant by instant. True or not, I sure wished I could have given it a whirl, added a few brushstrokes to the reality that was unfolding. I was certain that the true situation I was facing was only going to become more heated as Georgia lit up the pilot of her ire.

I watched as another man I'd known casually, and who went by the name of Hicks, moved close to Georgia.

"Every time I look at her I want to say the same thing," Hicks commented with a giant smile. He was referring to Cookie's attractiveness, whereas Georgia's "Holy shit!" exclamations were, unbeknownst to him, rather inspired by disbelief that Cookie and I were together and that I was violating her best friend. Hearing Hicks' lusting words about Cookie led Georgia to position herself in a confrontational pose, Hicks still not in the least understanding the source of her consternation.

"I tip my hat to the man," Hicks continued. "Hell, sometimes a man's gotta do what a man's gotta do."

"Yeah, I know some women who do what they gotta do too!" Georgia countered, notably irked.

"Sure, some women. But no woman I'd be with," Hicks declared.

"Of course not," Georgia moaned submissively. "I'm sure they're all just innocent Detroit girls."

"We're all innocent Detroit girls," one of the other ladies sung her way into the exchange.

By now Garland had lost interest in Georgia's antics. He seemed to want to defuse what he saw as an impending gender battle. He turned to walk away from Georgia. It was then that Angel Face, an entertainer that Garland had been trying to land, came over to greet him. They exchanged ritualistic hand clasping and hugs, but Angel Face seemed solemn. Eagerly, he led Garland away, notably to speak to the man alone.

I eyed them as they went to the far end of the room. Angel was entreating him with grim gestures. All the while, Garland appeared unfazed. It was like watching big papa telling his son there's not a thing to worry about and to calm down. After a few minutes, they again embraced. Angel seemed more relaxed, as if his confidence had been paroled from prison. That's when Garland called over to me, while dangling Angel Face like a Rolex watch on his wrist.

"Benny, I got someone I want you to meet."

"I think I know Angel. We've been introduced before," I reminded him as they continued to head my way.

Cookie loosened her grip on me, but stood close.

"Well, meet Angel again," Garland rejoiced. "He's up and coming up higher. And after I dine with him, I'm going to sign him. Ha, ha, fame's the name of the game, right my friends?"

"Definitely, we're working on that one, my man," responded what appeared to be a rejuvenated Angel Face, for after his comment, he and Garland shared a boisterous, gleeful, ceremonial series of hand gestures. All the while, neither of them could stop their heads from cocking in Cookie's direction.

"In case you didn't notice," Garland spoke to Angel, "this here is Cookie."

"Mama gave you the right name," Angel wafted her way.

"She said I popped out soft and sweet."

"Ha, ha. I like that," Angel smiled, now sounding like Garland.

"So, you're looking to be a star, Miss Cookie?" Angel had directed his full attention to her while Garland tried to occupy me with his vacuous joviality.

"In my own right, I'm a star already," Cookie beamed.

"Yes, I'd agree. But you could be bigger and bigger in a big hurry," Angel told her.

While Angel was trying to hustle Cookie, Hicks approached again.

"Hey, Angel, you ready to make beautiful music babies this week in the studio? I'm ready to get down on it, right Garland?"

"Hicks, you and Angel got...a little different style," Garland responded so as to not encourage a session he would never have allowed to take place.

"Yeah, I know. But we both make beautiful music babies, don't we Angel?"

"I'd like to see this lady's musical babies," Angel joked.

"Hey, Benny," Hicks tittered, completely dismissing Angel's reference to Cookie. "Me and Angel gonna make beautiful music babies this week."

"Sounds beautiful, Hicks," I remarked indifferently.

"Come over here," Hicks yelled to Georgia in a giggling voice. Since she first noticed us, Georgia had for obvious reasons been glaring at the encounters taking place between Cookie and me. "You know Benny?" Hicks asked.

"Lookee, lookee. What do we have here, Mr. Benny Wright?" Georgia hissed like a cat warning a dog it was about to have its eyes scratched out.

I took the cue. The best I could do was nod uncomfortably and say nothing. It was Georgia who raised her claws, pressing forward with the exchange while fixing Cookie in her sights.

"Why don't you introduce me to your...friend, Mr. Benny...Wright, isn't it?"

"Georgia, this is Cookie; Cookie, this is Georgia." I performed the introductions in a perfunctory manner, squaring off with Georgia for the dreaded disclosure I knew I had no choice but to reveal—my wife's buddy would have insisted I do so had I chosen to try and evade it. "Cookie, Georgia is Jewel's best friend."

What I'll never forget is that Cookie showed no sign of intimidation. She never said a word. Instead, she reached down for my hand like it was an old possession.

"Everything fine then, Mr. Wright?" Georgia snarled, itching for a war.

"Things are great," I answered.

"Great!" she blurted out.

Her sneer and vehemence reminded me a second time that dipping into my imagination, allowing me to fantasize a scene void of hostility, was a perfect solution.

I hadn't perfected the skill, or if I had, my witness state of mind refused to serve me. Thus, I awaited Georgia's attack. Fortunately, one of the other guests, a man I knew as a local music executive, Marlon, walked over to join the clutch of actors at center stage, now including Hicks, Garland, Georgia, Angel Face, and me. His agenda was pursuing justice. His intervention was favorable to me in that he diverted the discussion away from my being with Cookie.

"Let's be fair. A man has rights," Marlon decreed as if he were a spokesman for a league of male voters.

The last cast member I expected to jump into the fray was Angel Face. He was too young and fresh, I thought, to care about getting mixed up in a war of the sexes. But he surprised me, leaping intrepidly into a role he awarded himself.

"The man has a point," Angel Face proclaimed fiercely.

"Constitutional rights!" Georgia mocked, undaunted by the sweet-faced star.

"See ladies," Angel Face continued warmheartedly, gently swinging his hand in a circular motion to announce his intent to address all the women present, "men are a different breed. We're like water, always flowing gently."

"Oh, sounds so peaceful," Georgia swooned, but not without letting him know she was taunting him. "I see why they call you *The Angel*," she said in a whisperingly sweet voice.

"Indeed!" Angel smugly pursued his line of reasoning. "But...what if something dams us up and we can't run free? Then we're not so gentle. We start smacking around, trying to break free."

"I see," Georgia came back to him, but with an ingenuous display of empathy, one shared by the other ladies who had waltzed into the area to witness the scene. They all nodded their heads with sympathetic lip, mouth, and eye expressions.

"That's why the smart ladies know that once in a while he's gotta do what he's gotta do. It's our natcha," Angel angelically labeled the indomitable quirk of the male gender.

"Ya natcha?" Georgia sarcastically imitated his unabashed mispronunciation.

"Ya natcha?" the other ladies mimicked Georgia's slur.

"Listen up," Angel Face instructed his audience. "Now, sit back ladies," he began gently, "with a drink in the hand and listen real close so you can understand, the nature of the beast, the nature of the man, it ain't that pretty, but it's the way things stand. L. A. men take friends to the beach when back in the den there's a hen in heat. N. Y. fools use musicals to get out of the house, away from their jewels. In MA, they head up to Fenway. In LA, they dine with penne. In GA, they crack into crawfish and cake, but the story ends the exact same way. It's that simple I must say, it's that simple and anyway. If you missed any bit of the list get the gist, a perfect man will just never exist. Ladies," he lowered his voice to drive his point, "there's no such thing as a relationship unless the man's got some pie on the side."

The ladies teamed up to beat him down.

"We got it, it's all so clear. We got it, and we thank you dear. We got it, have no fear. We got it! We got it! An LA man takes his woman with a little suntan, we got that. Then the NY guy likes to have a little show on the side. We got that too. MA's, CA's and GA's all got a special way and they get away. We know it's true, and gentlemen, we'll be true too," they chuckled. "So sit back and get loose, we'd like to break some news.

"When you sin in Michigan, watch your back, you got that?! Sleep around in this little town and watch your back, you got that?! Do what you gotta, if you got the knack, but when you mess around in Michigan, watch your back."

There would have to be a finale. It was the ladies coming through, their obvious intent to put Angel Face's mug in the mud.

"You betta watch it, oh, you betta watch it." The ladies sung out in a soft harmony before laying down a harsh admonishment. "You got that?!!"

My now, having completed a piece I would have named "Detroit Women", all the girls were pointing their left index fingers at their men, serving notice that the Detroit crew didn't take kind to that element of man's "natcha."

137

*****

When the piece ended, the strangest thing happened. It would take me a bit of time before I could understand why the thoughts that popped into my head at that moment were there but they pertained to Dion, particularly regarding his conception. I wandered to a corner of the room to witness the spontaneous streaming of my mind's eye. The visions were grounded in a past reality. I was sure of that.

It began with me deliberating that I had never envisioned being a father. It was Jewel who had suggested that we have a family, a completely alien concept when she first mentioned it. I remember having little enthusiasm for the project and kept ignoring further discussion of it as much as possible.

Then as I replayed a mental track from the past, I realized that all the conflict I experienced at that time was likely similar to most men facing the same decision. I surmised as well that many men would have shared what took place within me the instant I saw my first child's birth. It took years before I realized that the entire structure of my being was remodeled in that one instant of becoming a father.

More memories. My love for Jewel before we started our family was without a doubt the deepest I had known. Yet I remember being aware and having a profound insight, as I witnessed Dion's birth, that something was different. I couldn't label the sensation with the same term, love, because the feelings I associated with what had just happened with Dion had a host of unique elements. I look back now and realize that when I saw that helpless little thing, as it lay on Jewel's chest, what had happened was that suddenly I'd been called to the highest service of mankind, parenthood.

In an instant, I grew up by a million years. I knew right then that Benny Wright had a purpose that would shadow him on every path he roamed, that would share in every breath he took, that would take a piece of every laugh, cheer, dance, song, and celebration he experienced. This purpose would be witness to every time he cheated, lied, or deceived; and gasp at every one of his sorrows, agonies, or defeats—there was something on earth that exceeded the worth of Benny Wright, that deserved his devotion until he was no longer a living being.

I was scared to death, that's how shell-shocked I was after Dion was born. But at Garland's party, my Perfect Plan was ironically reinforced by the recognition of the role I had assumed as a father. It was a role that I had sadly admitted failing at. That's when it hit me. It was why the material rising to the surface of my consciousness had been imposed on me at such an odd moment.

I was in attendance at Garland's with a secret mission to prove my devotion. I had taken the oath of fatherhood. I was dedicated to fulfilling it…one way or another, any way conceivable. I was in the process of making a public announcement on the point. I conceived Cookie as good fortune's ace of spades.

CHAPTER 11: GET OUT

All good things must come to an end. My marriage
to Jewel had been a good thing, but was it about to
come to a halt? It had been my intention to drive Jewel
away. Marital dissolution, however, was too overwhelming a thought to consciously contemplate.

As had been my new habit, I came in late each evening. It had been some time since the party at Garland's
house. Miraculously, Jewel still had no idea about the
gathering itself or that I had attended with my mystery
guest. Georgia had untypically kept a distance from
Jewel and made up excuses to not talk with her. It came
to the point that her friend wondered if quirky Georgia
was having as difficult a time as she was facing.

The truth was that dear Garland had advised her to
defer disclosing my association with Cookie. His position was that it was best to give the situation some time

to be sure it was an ongoing affair between Cookie and me before having a heart-to-heart with Jewel. Wily Garland, however, called Jewel during this period of time, attempting to begin weaseling his way into her life. In fact, the last guest at his party that evening hadn't even rolled out of his driveway before he was placing a just-thinking-about-you call to Jewel—who wouldn't call that friendship?

All the while, Jewel had decided that her best strategy would be to wait patiently. Benny was grieving about something bigger than a tragic, random murder. She resolved that eventually I'd come clean with whatever it was that had set an early mid-life crisis in motion. In the meantime, she convinced herself that the one unforgivable sin, unfaithfulness, wasn't the issue—her husband had denied it, and regardless of how much pain her man was in, the more she deliberated, the surer she was that his word was better than gold.

It was very early in the morning. Shana and Dion were still asleep. I was racing to make my shift at the plant. Jewel had decided to take another shot at what had her husband "by the horns." It might not have been the best time given that I was sleep deprived, due to my new schedule of staying out after work and not returning until late in the night. Nor was it a sign of good judgment to try and engage me in a discussion, when Jewel herself hadn't slept a complete night since my return home from New York that fateful evening—she had been moody and irritable with the children much more than ever before.

"Benny. I need a minute here. I know it hit you hard what happened with the young man being murdered in front of you. Look, you came home covered with blood; it must have been traumatic."

"Jewel, gotta go. I'll be late."

"Benny, do you expect me to live like this forever? We're a couple," she implored. "We've always talked to each other about everything and anything. That's what we have that's special."

I went into the kitchen to grab the packed lunch Jewel religiously prepared for me. I was holding my keys in my right hand and a toolbox in my left. I leaned my head downward toward the countertop and picked up the paper sack with my teeth. Jewel ran over and took it out of my mouth, walking by my side out to the car.

"Don't ruin this for us, Benny. I love you. I miss you," she entreated. "You want me to beg, humiliate myself? Okay, I'm desperate. I'll do anything you ask. You want to move? I'll go. We need money? I'll get a job. I'm not satisfying you sexually? Just tell me what you need," Jewel implored tearfully. "You name it. That's what I'll do to save us."

"I told you Jewel, there's nothing you can do. I gotta go."

"You swore when we decided to get married that you'd never cheat on me. Don't break that promise, goddamn it!" she spontaneously expressed, perplexed why she had spoken the words.

I jumped into the car and stormed off. Two blocks from my house, I pulled over. I thought I was going to pass out. Jewel is a strong lady, stronger than even I had imagined. I knew it would take time to break her down before she'd kick me out, but this was unthinkable. Nobody should be asked to inflict torture on someone they love. Yet, for her good, I had no choice.

I can imagine any sane person wanting to beat some sense into me. "Why don't you simply man-up and leave?" The answer is that I knew my wife. Jewel would have never moved on to someone else until she had rid herself of me. If I left, she'd keep waiting for me to come back—she's as loyal as water is wet.

I finally pulled myself together and went on to work. It seemed that once I was engaged with my new life outside the home I was okay. I could divorce myself from the struggle with Jewel. I had never contemplated how I'd handle it on a more permanent basis, but I was about to find out—the wish for Jewel to put an end to her devotion to me was about to be realized.

I recall the exact date that it happened. It was the afternoon of June 23rd. Jewel was tidying up the family room, when Shana came in from school. She was in a happy mood, humming a song she'd been listening to endlessly.

"Come now, get some real feel music; bum around to

144

some real feel music," she sang as she flung her back-pack like a worthless sack toward her section of the common space. "Hi, Mom," she greeted as she continued her lyrics. "It's that simple when you got a smooth lick, a bumpin' bass line and some drums that kick, a little bit of Ella, some Snoop..."

"Shana, what's that you're singing?" Jewel asked, intrigued by the words.

"Oh my God, you are out of it, Mom. It's called music," she lightly admonished with a "wake up" sort of tone.

Their conversation was interrupted when the doorbell rang.

"Please get it, Shana," Jewel instructed, battling the remnant drippings of ice cream that Dion had left on the coffee table the night before.

Shana answered the door while still humming her tune. Unexpectedly, it was Georgia. As she smiled at the fun lady friend of her mom, the words flowed out, "Come now get some real feel music, bum..."

"Around to some real feel music, come now get some real feel music in your life, it feels so right," Georgia sang along with Shana.

Georgia gave Shana a hug. As she did, it was apparent her joyous tone dropped as fast as her handbag, which landed on a chair.

"Shana, let Mommy and I talk. Go on, scat," she said as she playfully whisked her hand, gesturing for the girl to leave.

Jewel saw the strain coming to Georgia's face and let loose of the rag she was using to clean. She came over to see what was wrong with her friend.

"Something happened?"

"Maybe you better be taking a seat, honey," Georgia signaled by pointing ominously to a chair.

Jewel didn't have a second to follow the eerie instruction. Garland entered the front door—he wouldn't have missed the pleasure of dropping a bomb on Jewel, especially one that he knew would weaken her to the point he could make a play for her.

"Door was open, so I let myself in." Then he looked at Georgia and addressed her. "You told her?"

"Said I'd wait for you, didn't I?"

"Told her what?" Jewel shrieked, anticipating trauma.

"Oh shucks, you're the king when it comes to tearing out hearts, you tell her," Georgia said flippantly, eager to grant the honor to Garland.

"I had a little party for friends and associates a week or so ago…and Benny showed up…with a girl…Cookie's the name."

"She was smothering him like mascara on a zit…right in front of all of us." Georgia's eyes closed and her hands found themselves grasping her hips. "I was an inch from gouging out her eyeballs, ripping out his sacred 'jewels'… then doing me some real redecorating."

"Jewel, I didn't want you to get hurt." Garland voiced with more sensitivity than he could earnestly express.

"Just go on, Garland," Jewel commanded.

"He's been seen one place after another with her since then. I had to tell you. Georgia and I didn't want you to find out some other way."

"I knew it," she said in a subdued tone. "I knew it!" she repeated, with slowly evolving anger. "He lied to me; I asked him and he lied," she cried out with rage. "The one thing...I can't believe it!"

Garland reached out to take her hand, offering contrition that rightly would have come from me. "I couldn't stand what he was doing to you."

"Another woman; it's the one thing I won't tolerate."

"You need anything, anything, I'll be there in an instant. You know that, Jewel, right?" Garland offered.

"Just go now. I need to be alone."

Both Garland and Georgia were eager to be on their way, but the worst-case scenario happened before they could escape. Benny Wright returned early to the house.

I was so hurried when I left that morning that I had forgotten to take clothes for the evening. I thought I'd sneak in and out real quietly, hoping Jewel would be out running errands. It was bad...bad timing. But to tell the truth, it had to happen—I willed it all along and was glad to get it over with.

I hung my coat and laid down the brown sack containing what I hadn't eaten of my lunch. Facing me was a grim-faced wife.

"Benny?" Garland fumbled.

I stared at him but I said nothing.

"Well then. Jewel, Benny, y'all take care now. I gotta go do a whole lot and then a whole lot more. Busy afternoon, you know. Georgia's got a lot to do too. I'm sure y'all got stuff to sort out anyway. Don't need us arou…" Garland stumbled out the words; Georgia was unable to speak.

They both made a quick beeline to the front door and dashed out. Jewel had already decided her course of action.

"Why, Benny?" she shouted. "Why, Benny? Why?" she demanded in a still louder voice.

"Why what?" I responded indifferently.

"I always told you any malicious, vicious, poisonous truth is better than a lie. But you had to deceive me."

"Someday you'll…"

"Today, Benny, today!" she hollered. "Today you get the hell out of here—for good! It's time to get packed," Jewel's words fitting like a wrench strangling the throat of a pipe.

I'll never forget this moment; nobody would. Dion and Shana had come in from their rooms. There were the three most precious people in my life engaged in a battle over how to handle my deceit. Jewel had run out of the room and returned with a suitcase. Then she kept coming back from our room with handfuls of clothing that she stuffed into the case. The children had a different idea, trying to take out the items as quickly as Jewel packed them. It was a tug of war, one where Jewel vastly overpowered her children. She managed to stuff the case full and latch it. All the while she was vehemently shouting her thoughts at me, doing it lyrically. "It's Time to Get Packed" is the title I'd give to her words.

"I was worried, and I was concerned. I was lonely, but I stood firm." She clenched her jaw, placing her hands on her hips, looking down at the empty suitcase she'd dropped on the floor. "I was just saddened and pitying you. I couldn't fathom the things you would do. What was I feeling? Sour and confused, but I figured in hours it would feel like a ruse. If you'd explain the thoughts in your brain, I'd know I was the same and you were in pain. But then things changed—today! Now I'm livid and I'm inflamed. On the hit of a button, all of a sudden I heard four words that shocked me and burned me right to a fume."

Dion had picked up the case, attempting to remove it from the scene. She was pulling back against his strength, yanking so hard that Dion nearly fell over. Then she addressed me in the most hateful tone.

"Know what those words were? *Benny cheated on you!* Before I was just bent but now I've been cracked, so it's time to get packed and that's that. I was just scared, but now I'll fight back. I was unsteady, but now I'm unlatched, so get packed."

The tirade continued, as if she were trying to spit out poison from her bowels.

"Leave, it's my family now. I don't care what you do but don't come back around. Go play with that little damn toy of yours. Buy it jewelry and tell it stories, take it on vacation, kiss it like a child…'cause these lips, they're not on file.

Shana, gushing tears, pled with her mom. "Mom, no. Don't make Daddy go."

Dion was shameless as well. "Don't make him go, Mom. Don't give up, Mom."

Their cause was hopeless. "Sorry kids. I'm simply enraged. My anger's uncaged." Then she looked at me with disgust. "So you better gauge your best course of action. I'd get packin', and I'm not askin'" The final words had to leave no doubt as to the finality of her position in the minds of her children or myself. "Get out!!!"

Jewel carried the now-closed suitcase to the front door, motioning for me to leave. She paused. Then she glanced to the corner of the room where the umbrellas were sitting in the canister. She reached and took one out, tossing it to me. I stared back bewilderedly after catching it in my right hand, my left lifting the suitcase.

I exited to the definitive slam of a mean door. The children were standing in shock. With authority and decisiveness, Jewel faced her children.

"Dion," she barked, "help me vacuum the living room!"

I stood outside the door of my own house. It felt like an end of something.

"What a lucky guy," I jested to myself. But it wasn't

luck at all. It was one hell of a job well done, just like my perfect plan predicted. I deserved to take a bow but had no appetite for accolades.

CHAPTER 12: STEPPING OUT

Most men would be in a funk after being tossed out like trash by their wife. Obviously, under the circumstances, it would be expected to be cause for rejoicing by me. But was it? Could I say that I didn't have mixed feelings? When it finally happened, I had more doubts than I wanted to admit. But I went back to my heart, the spirit of nobility and love that inspired me from the beginning, the words of the dying man—that's where I found solace.

I remember right after I was left standing on the porch, I picked up the suitcase and moved to the sidewalk. I peered back toward the house, but neither Jewel nor the children were looking out. It was a bit stunning to me. I thought they might be wondering what I was going to do but instead the family room was empty. That tore at my gut. Still, I stayed the course. At that point, I really had no choice.

I did the right thing. Hell, it was "guaranteed to succeed." Death, taxes, perverts on the Internet, Harvard University with no debt, and the plan of Benny Wright, all things guaranteed.

On the street those words, "guaranteed to succeed," sounded in my head and I smiled mysteriously. Then I started humming the tune with that name,

"Guarant e e d To Succ e e d."

I put the suitcase down on the street. In a meditative, contemplative, musing tone, what could have been an a capella rehash of the words I spoke at Jimbo's when I first hit upon my "guarant e e d to succ e e d plan, I unconsciously and spontaneously spoke a subtle message of uncertainty.

"It's guarant e e d to succ e e d, and that's the way things'll be. Just like the days pass quick and become the past, and the flies get busy in the summertime grass. Ladies want love without a question asked, and indeed it draws a fight when the dream gets crashed. Just like the strings of a symphony shake when they move, and the trombones blast out melodic tunes. People get calm to the sound of the flutes, and my wife loves to speak 'til I'm mute."

I wasn't teary, but I wasn't rejoicing either as more words poured out.

"A little bit of luxury is okay. A little bit of gold

dangling cold on a chain; a little bit of trips to the mall makes you sane. A little bit that's it. Why am I in a little bit of pain? It's guaranteed, I'll shout, without a bit of doubt. I'm not even a little bit concerned that she's a little bit put out. It's guarant e e d to succ e e d, and that's just the way thing'll be."

When I finished the last muse, I picked up my meager possessions. I had already scouted out a place to go when the inevitable happened, so I went immediately to my new quarters. It was a shithole of an apartment, if I may put it bluntly. Looking back, I think I had a need to inflict punishment on myself. The squalid conditions that I chose to live in were just the first lash of a whip on my flesh.

The unit I chose was in Oakwood Heights, not too far from my home. It was tiny and in a rundown building, but I didn't mind. It was a sacrifice worth making, at least for the "short run," until Jewel found a man to take up with.

One of the variables that I'd failed to account for was the length of time it might take before Jewel was ready to entertain the concept of a new lover. I kept dismissing it as a minor flaw in my plan. In the meantime, I had to live my life. One of the things I noticed was that I started volunteering for every extra shift I could get. If one of the guys was ill or had to take off for a family emergency, I grabbed his hours. There was no doubt that I was working off tension, but to my thinking I was teaching boredom that it couldn't bully me.

I also made sure I was seen with Cookie. I didn't want there to be any doubts in Jewel's mind that we might reunite. I spent increasingly greater amounts of time getting to know Simon better. In fact, it was right after Jewel put me out of the house that I disclosed to him the brilliance of what I was doing as well as the history necessitating the implementation of my plan. I was hesitant to share it with him and I was shocked by how he responded.

He stood up and hugged me warmly. Then he stared into my eyes with an intensity that I'd never before experienced.

"I'm sorry you were so tragically hurt," was all he said.

The openings of his eyes narrowed. I witnessed wetness filming on his corneas.

"I'll do the crying for you, Benny."

"I did the right thing, Simon. I had no choice, right?"

He didn't say a word, just tilted his head and with the gentlest sigh, leaned back in his chair in a contemplative pose. His eyes remained shut for some time. His face reflected grief greater than what I was aware of experiencing myself in that moment. Finally, he looked at me again, still speechless.

I was confused by his reaction, unnerved is more accurate. It raised the level of doubt already in my mind.

As I stared at him, I suddenly wanted his approval, a simple statement that I had acted with wisdom.

"You never answered if you think I did right."

"It's not important what I think," he said kindly. "I respect you. Your love will prevail in the end."

"It is the end, Simon."

Why my words were so entertaining I had no idea, but his face did an about-face from the gloominess of a moment earlier, now taking on a glow as he laughed himself silly.

"After Cookie and I..."

"Huh," he shrugged.

I don't know what he was forecasting for the future but it wasn't in line with my thoughts.

"Some people will die for their family. You have made the ultimate sacrifice. You'll see what's going to happen."

"What? I'll see what?" I anxiously queried him.

"We'll get to it."

In an instant, the sorrow returned to his face. Then Simon reached into his jacket and took out a pen. On the table was a small napkin. He wrote his name, "Simon Ritter," followed by two phone numbers—his cell and home line. After he handed it to me, he stood up.

"You call me, any time, day or night. I never thought I'd meet another man as wild as myself. I'm proud to have you as a friend."

Then he left. It was the first time I'd seen him walk

in a weary shuffle, the normal spring and energy of his gait absent.

I sat for over an hour, unsure how to read what had occurred. He appeared more pained than I, and it wasn't even his life.

During the next few months, I'd see him frequently. He never asked me how things were progressing with Jewel and the children. That was a wise approach because it wasn't going pleasantly. Not infrequently I'd receive furious calls from Jewel demanding money—she had no other topic to discuss with me and evaded answering my questions pertaining to Dion and Shana. At first, I'd send just enough to keep her afloat, in order to pay the basic bills and to sustain her and the children.

Then, as time went on, it dawned on me that unless the pressure intensified she'd not entertain advances from qualified suitors. That's when I decided to reduce the stream of money to a trickle. The strategy resulted in even more enraged calls; then randomly interspersed, I'd find frantic voice messages on my cell. These graduated from making me aware that she was getting calls from bill collectors to notifying me that she was going to lose the house if she didn't make the mortgage payments. I ignored the pleas, based on my newly born belief that if she was too comfortable financially, she wouldn't be inclined to take up with a man who would accomplish for her what I had failed to do.

I can't help but recall in particular one occasion when

Jewel showed up as I was leaving work, shouting at me while tears streamed down her face. The rant was over her having found a job but still being under duress to meet the monetary demands of the family. Heartlessly, I jumped into my car and left her standing in the lot.

How could I have been so cold and cruel? That's the unfathomable question that I'm still not able to resolve. All I can conclude is that I had sold myself on the belief that love took many forms, one type necessitating a person to do what was the right thing even though they might die doing it.

Simon listened attentively to my accounting of these events as they transpired between Jewel and me. He encouraged me to talk to him, and I never once sensed he was judging me. He was all about empathy and genuine regard for what I was experiencing, which I found myself expressing to him more freely.

He'd often be teary. The man was true to his pledge that he'd do the crying for me. He was especially bountiful with emotion when I shared with him the moments of nightmare and anguish I'd have, interspersed with the sensations of pure gratification I felt knowing that my family would be rewarded in the end.

Between work, Cookie, Jimbo's, and Simon, I managed to exist while my family adjusted to life without me. I stayed as far away from them as I could. It wasn't a problem since with the exception of financial assistance, Jewel wanted as much to do with me as a coiled rattler.

CHAPTER13: LET'S DO LOVE

While I was dissolving as a force in my family's life, Garland was doing what he'd not spent a night *not doing* since high school, imagining himself with my wife. The fact is that he had built her up in his mind as a diva, the leading lady in his world of fantasy, a precious amulet stolen from him out of the asphalt playground in our neighborhood by a dreamer with no future, Benny Wright.

How had it happened that he, Garland, a top-of-the-world guy in a top-of-the-world industry, had to play second fiddle to a man who inspected car parts during the day and wrote songs, not really worth even a dime, in the evening? Garland had been a friend of mine since childhood. While I'm certain he knew I had talent, I doubt now that he ever had much conflict about whether he'd devote himself to assisting or destroying my career pursuits. The latter category had to have dominated his will and likely in the end, sealed my fate.

I'd known all along that he couldn't wipe away the never-ceasing drool he had for the most darling girl he'd ever seen in his life—he idolized Jewel. Now, at long last, I was out of the picture. From the second he saw me with Cookie, he was in a state of delight. My infidelity permitted him to judge me as being indisputably no more than a contemptible rascal. He could point out to Jewel that had she seen it from the beginning, she wouldn't be suffering in her life as she was now. In the same breath, he could assure her that it was possible for her error in judgment to be forgiven later. The goal for Garland, while I ignored Jewel's demands for financial assistance, was to woo her into his life.

Routinely during those months, he'd show up and bring gifts, for both Jewel and the children. She'd refuse his offers to step in and help with money but he never gave up. He'd invite her to go to his clients' concerts, and when she'd flatter him with an acceptance, he'd haul Dion and Shana along with them. Anytime he knew where she was, he'd show up unexpectedly, and if she were working he'd sometimes arrive as she was leaving to relieve her from having to use the bus.

He was apprised of her financial struggles. She never hesitated to bring up the topic of funds. She was holding down a job, but the ends she was trying to meet were stretched too far for her to connect them together. It caused her to berate me in front of him all the more caustically for not sending her money. It was a simple calculation that even an imbecile could have made, determining that she wouldn't have enough to pay her bills.

She hadn't misled me when she said she had no choice but to neglect making the house payment and further that she had already received a first notice of delinquency. Her parents were poor and wouldn't have been able to help, even if she could have waived her pride and gone to them.

Making matters all the more favorable for the scheming Garland was that Jewel's job was not stable. Some weeks, her hours were cut and at other times, she was told not even to come in. She tried to supplement the trickling income stream with part-time temporary jobs, but they were scarce due to the declining economy.

Over time, she began to panic. Her emotions were only a notch beneath the threshold of desperation—Garland was a shark and smelled the blood before it poured from her veins. Jewel would never let on to the children about what she was going through. In the fatherless Wright family, all seemed normal on the surface. Jewel was a woman who knew that sometimes "a woman has to do what a woman has to do" and she never hesitated doing whatever was necessary for the care of her loved ones.

The children didn't look too happy. However, under the stern mastery of their mom they were handling their homework and keeping up the pretense of pride—Jewel would have never permitted them to mope or weep. As urgent as she realized the situation was, she held her head up in the presence of her children.

She wanted her offspring to understand that even when facing circumstances of gross betrayal, one had to have dignity. If a person had a cause to fight for, then if necessary, they were expected to put their heart and soul on the line to win. Even if the battle was lost, the only choice was to stand tall. The sole concession she allowed in defeat was to bow to the victor, in this case a malignant cell that had mortally inflicted a man of weak character, a man named Benny Wright…who cheated.

While Shana and Dion were doing their homework and preparing for dinner, a haggard Jewel, dressed in a skirt and high heels, walked in. She threw her coat and purse on the sofa. Shana was sitting at the kitchen table reading a book.

"Shana, is the pasta boiling?" Jewel was grumpy but covered her true feelings with a costumed smile.

"Almost. Why are you home so late?" Shana questioned with a tone that seemed mildly reproving.

"It's called a job, love." Jewel grimaced.

"You never worked before," Shana scorned. "Where's Daddy?"

"Shana, how many times do we have to go over this? Your father decided to leave us."

The salad that Jewel had prepared before heading

off to work was in the refrigerator. Dion walked over and took it out. With mechanical motions, he placed the wood bowl on the counter, poured in dressing, and tossed the ingredients.

"You kicked him out," Shana charged. "I was right here, and so was Dion. Right, Dion?"

"She's right, Mom," he answered woefully, never looking at Jewel.

"It's been weeks." Shana routinely calendared the statistic for her mom.

"Try months," Dion added, shameless to commit a small act of exaggeration.

It was well into summer and Detroit was sizzling under a heat wave—the Wright family was in a boil.

"Shana. Dion. I told you both a person has to do what's right sometimes, even though it hurts."

"Maybe Daddy did what he thought was right," Dion posed.

"Defend your father?" Jewel bristled. "No, Dion. Your father did what felt was good for…himself only."

"Sometimes you have to forgive, Mom. That's what you tell us all the time."

"Dion, he's not asking for forgiveness."

"Well, the way I see it, all you have to do is let him come back." Dion retorted, still avoiding eye contact. That he was intolerant of his mom was evident by the sneer on his face.

"Let him come back?! Someday you'll learn, son, and

I hope not the hard way, that without honesty and integrity a relationship is like a boat with a leak in the middle of the sea. It has to sink, and if you don't get off you're sure to perish. Well, I'm not going to drown," she declared, her consternation powerful enough to suppress the tears that were competing for expression. "I have two children to take care of," she finally shrieked. "Where is your father? Go ask him!"

Dion finished his task and placed the bowl on the table. Shana proceeded as if the conversation were just beginning. She stood up and began motoring around the table.

"Well, I think this is all a big waste of time. According to a very reliable site on the Internet, sixty-seven percent of marriages at one time or another have a separation. Forty-nine percent of the time someone cheats. But out of all the time someone is unfaithful, only a third of the people get a divorce." She paused to read her audience. "See what I'm saying?"

For the first time, Dion looked at his mother, trying to mask a smile, the same one Jewel was battling.

"Two-thirds of the people work it out." Shana reached appealingly to take her mom's hands in hers. "And people like you, who have been married for so long and have children, have even a better chance to resolve their differences." She stopped to look imploringly at her Mom. "So what I think is that if you and Daddy sat down and talked it out, he could come home."

The world of a child, even a genius child with insight and understanding years beyond her chronological age, is a universe of Play dough that can be shaped at will into any form or object. It's a blessed state, stolen heartlessly by the winding wheels, pins, and springs of a cruel timekeeper. Shana was an extraordinary example of a young girl who used the vastness of her imagination to reposition the key players in the script she was writing to create a painless outcome—sadly, the power of children falls flat on its face in an adult cosmos.

Jewel knew that. She was spared the task of breaking her child's heart for the thousandth time since she showed me the door. In fact, it was the door that saved her. The bell rang. Dion ran over to see whom it was.

It was Garland. As usual, he was smiling wide as a runway. In his hands, were parcels with clothing items he'd purchased to surprise Jewel—treats for her and the children he was confident that eventually she'd accept. Already he'd been pleading with her to let him do more—the urgency of her situation was bankrupting Jewel's pride.

Garland shook hands with the little man and waved to Shana.

"I'm sorry, Garland. I got home a bit late. Did you eat?"

"I'm fine, darlin'. Hey, Dion. How's that album coming? I'm waitin' to make you a star," he chuckled.

"Shoot, Garland. In three years, I'll be too big for you to sign," Dion quipped.

165

Garland responded in a happy-go-lucky manner. "Ha, ha! Then talk to me in two and a half."

"Dion, Shana, go clean yourselves up and we'll eat in a bit. It's time for grownup talk."

"That sucks, Mom," Shana growled.

"That double sucks," Dion dittoed.

Garland and Jewel talked while Shana and Dion moved across the room. Dion put his earphones on Shana, wanting her to listen to the music he'd recently written. She was grooving to the sound and Dion was writing in a composition book. They were engrossed in what they were doing, paying no attention to Garland and their mom.

"Well...did you think about it?" Garland asked sweetly.

"I just don't see how I can," Jewel responded soberly.

"You can't make it work, not all alone. Can't you see that?" he pled his case. "With those children and all they need...all alone you can't...can't you see?"

"Garland..."

"No, those children need things, things that I can give them, that I want to give them. Hell, Jewel, they're special. If you don't give them the opportunity they'll never fulfill their potential," he tactfully reasoned.

"Those children are not yours. You have no responsibility for them and you know it."

"I want the responsibility...and I don't want to remind

166

you that their irresponsible father has dropped it. Jewel, he's selfishly starving you."

"Besides, Garland, the children won't have it. It won't work, that's all."

"Things will take a little time, sure," he pitched. "But they'll get over it and they'll get used to me." Garland paused to look as earnest as he was capable of conveying to the woman who enthralled him. "Jewel, I've loved you forever. I should have never let you go."

"You didn't. I wasn't in love with you...I loved Benny," she spontaneously corrected him.

"Well, Benny's a cheat...an undependable cheat. Not like me."

"This is just all happening so fast. I can't keep up. It's not...right. No, Garland, I'm married," she said mournfully. "I could never..."

"Then we'll wait until you're divorced. Getting...cozy isn't everything. Just having you close to me means the world."

"Garland, it would only be for convenience. It's not fair to you," she fought back.

"It's fair," he said flatly, pausing to punctuate the point. "We need to be together. We need each other."

"I need love," she stated in a hushed voice.

While Garland was seducing my wife, Dion and Shana were sharing music; at least until hunger challenged their patience. In order to intrude on the adult talk, Dion intentionally cranked up a beat but instead

167

of becoming upset on the spot, Garland hit it with lyrics. Dion couldn't believe it. The man represented artists, but after hearing him, my son was convinced Garland in the past might have been an entertainer as well. Spontaneously he was laying it out, smoothly dropping words to Dion's beat. The best name for the piece would be "Let's Do Love."

"We fit like water and food, you'll see the harmony brew. Let's do love, it's the sensible thing to do. I'll be true, you'll see the harmony brew, let's do love, it's the sensible thing to do. Now I know you want to take it slow, but it is right I simply know, I'm at one with this house, and I feel so close. Don't deny us as a pair, it's a special thing that's rare, take me into this life and do as you care. It's a beautiful fit and more, the perfect square of four, and when those children need me, I'll be there in a storm."

The con artist was about to close the deal.

"Now listen to me, Jewel. I don't want to sound cold, and I don't want to sound insensitive. I know you've got your hang ups, and I've got mine too. But can't you see the harmony, Jewel? I'm right on the same page as all of you."

His lines were inspiration, but only to Garland. In truth, all he was doing was spinning prattle, unintentionally creating farce. Most of the time he was singing, his eyes stayed closed or he had his back turned from Jewel. While he was proclaiming the "harmony" of them

168

being on the same page and advancing other arguments that supported them becoming a family, he was paying no attention to the real dynamic that had taken place between Jewel and her children.

"You fall, I feel the floor shake," he beseeched at one point.

As he spoke those words, Dion and Shana took to fighting over a rubber stretch exerciser, each pulling mightily for possession. All of a sudden, Dion intentionally let go, which caused Shana to fall and hit her nose on the end of a table. Jewel ran over to her and took a tissue from her pocket, holding it to Shana's bleeding nose.

"You bleed, I see red," Garland declared, unaware of the mini-tragedy unfolding.

Jewel had by then secured a piece of Kleenex under Shana's upper lip.

"You need a helping hand, and mine's there to take," Garland vowed.

The bleeding under control, Shana looked for payback. She aimed a solid poke at Dion's eye, causing Jewel to again intervene, chewing out the children for playing in the house. Dion was peeved.

"Things get hectic, and I'm right there for you," Garland vowed during the worst of the commotion.

As the scene between the children calmed, Jewel walked back to where Garland was executing the final touches of his soliloquy. She stared at him for a moment before he turned to view her. He was still unaware of what had transpired between her and the children. Jewel picked up a glass of water and placed a pill in her mouth.

"Excuse me?" Jewel was puzzled, but the show wasn't over. Dion, teed off, raised the volume of the music far above where it had started. Garland didn't even wait for Jewel to swallow, repeating some of his lyrics in prose.

"Jewel," he beseeched, "we fit like water and food, you'll see the harmony brew, let's do love, it's the sensible thing to do. Jewel, darlin', I'll be true and you'll see the harmony brew...so let's love, it's the sensible thing to do."

Still facing Jewel, while intensely peering into her eyes, he waited several seconds before locking down the deal.

"If you won't come live with me then at least let me stay here sometimes in the guest room. It's a way to start. I won't take no for an answer."

In return, Jewel fixed her gaze on him. She looked as if she were inspecting his sanity. Then, she tentatively nodded several tiny movements of her head up and down before mouthing one time, "okay."

Wow! Wow! Wow! That's what any rational soul had to be thinking. *Wow!* I had fully accepted my harsh title: Benny Wright, Biggest Fool, Class of '94? But...Jewel Wright, Biggest Sap, Class of Broken Hearts, 2012? *Really?*

My wife was a beautiful woman, not only her physical

self but also her inner being. She had all the traits that any man would find priceless. She was proud to a flaw, strong in her faith, gutsy, untiring in defending her family, and she was courageous to do anything necessary to secure love in her life.

Garland? Garland? Garland? I kept asking myself how this lady—in the land of hot fudge sundaes with whipped cream, nuts, and a sweet cherry reclining atop—could in the end, after battling the illogic of a man she knew was as FOS as soda pop makers boasting about the healthiness of soft drinks for children, acquiesce like a jellyfish, opening the way for him to eventually secure a full-time presence in her life. As I mentioned, I knew he loved her all along, but never in my wildest imagination would I have thought it would be Garland she'd surrender to.

Then, as I deliberated the unimaginable, a giant sign dropped out of the sky of my consciousness, a jeering banner ironically inscribed as a dedication. *MORON.* That's all it said, except in the corner in small print was the name: Benny Wright.

My head was rotating like a top; I'll admit it. I couldn't make sense out of senselessness. Was I missing something that was obviously sensible?

"Moron, moron, moron," I repeated, wondering who was sending the message and why. Was it some supernatural authority that was responsible for bringing the banner on stage? Was it a prop that was supposed to ramp up my imagination by giving me a mirthful jab in the rib? Worse, was it a forewarning of the ultimate punishment that I anticipated coming my way?

I massaged all these ghastly thoughts one day as I talked it through with Simon. He continued encouraging me to freely express whatever was roaming around in my head but he refrained from attempting to have any influence. During one of our sessions, I had an instant of clarity. It emerged from the muddle of material that had been swirling in my mind—it quickly gained fist force, punching the answer in my face.

"I got it, Simon," I exalted. "Why did Jewel consent to toss in the towel and capitulate to the blatantly ingenuous appeal of Garland? I am a moron. I earned the title but only for not having seen it sooner."

"Go ahead. I'm listening," he urged me like a pal.

"It all begins with the children and their futures. Jewel would do anything to advance their lives. At the end of her existence, when she's due to meet her maker, she wants to die being able to report that she did everything in her living power to give them something to use to further their lives beyond what she'd accomplished with hers.

"Jewel shared with me the silent oath she took during her pregnancies that she would protect and defend her offspring to her last breath. What she swore to her God was unlimited, unconditional, and unalterable. She would perish for those two beings.

"When Garland laid out his proposal to her she had to be gazing her mind's eye into each of her children's faces, not Garland's," I assured Simon. "Absolutely, he's as shallow as a spilled cup of tea and as unfailing as a promise. But Garland could rescue her babes. He had everything they needed at that point to storm the world with the gifts that fate had given them. By-golly, she'd lay down like a whore, if she had to, in order to fulfill the promise she made at birth to each of them. No wonder, Simon, I couldn't figure it out when Craig first informed me what was happening between Jewel and Garland. I didn't want to see it," I declared.

"Simon, at some point she had to break under the pressure. Garland knew it all along." Then, my sense of astonishment peaked. "My Lord," I exclaimed loud enough that the rest of the customers glanced my way. "Jewel Wright is a carbon copy of...me."

I didn't know whether to blow my brain out or to rejoice in my revelation. Both Jewel and I shared, to the same extreme degree, that simple wish for our children. We had both endorsed it. I had signed off on it like a contract. Not being able to fulfill my end of the deal was disastrous for me. Jewel also wanted success for our children and would go to any extent to accomplish it. It was only anger to the degree I had driven her, however, that landed her in the clutches of Garland.

"You're right, Benny. Absolutely. Do you see what's happening now?" Simon asked.

"What do you mean?"

"Now your passion is teaming with wisdom. What to do next will come to you…you'll see," Simon ominously forecasted.

"My plan was genius, I have to admit it. This is everything I'd hoped for from the onset. I guess I have every reason to be jubilant." Then I looked over at Simon who was sitting across from me. "There is nothing next to do," I exclaimed.

It was another of those occasions when I could see that Simon was deeply hurting. The problem was that this time, so was I. My plan had graduated from perfect to immaculate; too good to be true. I could have never seen what was coming, but I believe now that Simon read trouble all the way.

To make matters worse, another tragic event was unfolding while dear Garland conveniently filled in the final piece of the puzzle that I'd orchestrated. It had been brewing for some time. Link's advocacy for the working man, born from the beat he wrote that inspired so many of the patrons at Jimbo's that day, couldn't be defused by the sole dissenting voice of rationalism. To the contrary, my friend became increasingly more zealous about his project, deciding that before music could accomplish its divine goal of proletariat liberation, he needed to have an organization to broadcast his platform.

He envisioned a movement with real muscle, as opposed to the existing teamster union groups that, in his opinion, were no different than lap dancers enjoying tips from rich customers. In this case, the clientele were top management who he believed were snugly in bed with the leaders of the unions, and at the expense of the workers who were funding their fling with dues. Where, or why, Link's mission came to be in the first place was a mystery to me.

Link had been brought up in a middle-class home. During the early years, he had always been shallow, in my opinion. He had furiously clung to his adolescent spirit. But then, all of a sudden, in what seemed like an instant, a metamorphosis took place. From that moment forward, he devoted every second of his existence, both while working and afterward, rallying troops to protest the "clowns" now "raiding" rather than "running" the established organizations, "supposedly" representing the workers.

His early success in his new endeavor was apparent. I witnessed it. People constantly sought him out to discuss Internet chatter, scheduled meetings for marketing and strategic plans to be used to crush the existing structure—then, as seems to be the case with any collection of people promoting a cause, eventually the evolving beast as a whole and united unit hungers for action, violently if necessary, to gain attention.

Link had been inciting hostility on the part of his followers over the course of a few months. There were frequent gatherings to discuss the most contentious issues, all the while the numbers throwing themselves behind him increased weekly. Several times the leaders of the union contacted him in an attempt to negotiate a merger. Link rebuffed them.

He finally called for a full demonstration outside the factory. I was never inclined toward politics, and was off work the day of the rally. However, I was told that several hundred followers had gathered to hear Link speak. Sadly, there was an unexpected glitch. Management ordered the group off the grounds, implying retaliation toward those who refused. As a result, after a prolonged standoff, most of the men wisely disbanded—realizing they might wake up to a notice of suspension or dismissal and then have to face a wife fiercer than the goons that management had brought out to intimidate the rioters.

Link was irate, trying to incite the remaining crew to battle the "thugs." Finally, the police were called out and with their assistance the group was broken up. However, the incident only sparked Link's increased wrath. He redoubled his efforts, ridiculed the "sissies" that had abandoned him, and at the same time called for stronger action.

It would have been a blessing had he been suspended, or even terminated. Instead, either management or the union—or both together—determined that the opposition Link was provoking, a virulent growth they had tried to nip in the bud, required a single cleaver blow to sever the head from the body. Thus, one evening after Link finished his shift, he walked with several of his buddies to his vehicle. On his way home, he stopped off at a convenience store to pick up a couple of items. It was dark and he had parked at the far end of the lot. He didn't have a chance to see what was coming, but in a flash a gang of men toting clubs and wearing steel-toed shoes descended on him.

Later that night, I received a call on my cell from Craig.

"You won't believe it," Craig panted urgently. "Link... they beat the crap out of him so bad...he's in the hospital."

"Who? Why?" I asked innocently.

"It had to be the company...or the union. Damn, I told him to back down," Craig remarked with notable exasperation.

"How bad is it?"

"Real bad. I talked to his mother. I'm on my way to the hospital. Want me to pick you up?"

"Of course."

Glancing into the hospital room from outside the door, when Craig and I saw Link, we both felt like vomiting. His cheeks looked like baseballs and his closed eyes popped out like a frog's. The doctors had performed some sort of light wiring of his jaw as a precaution, though it wasn't as badly injured as it could have been. He had bruising and welts all along his arms as well as visible abrasions on the sides of his neck. It was not his intent to do so, but Link's body served as evidence supporting those who argue that if you have to defend yourself, you'll fare better with brass knuckles and a steel club than the sound of Pete Seeger singing about civil and labor rights in "We Shall Overcome." Link had lost the fight badly, but his argument that music was the common man's ally was still not without merit.

Craig and I finally entered the room. We said hello to Link, hoping he could hear. The poor man could hardly acknowledge us. He couldn't talk but motioned at one point for us to come closer; he whispered like a ventriloquist with laryngitis.

"At least I fought for what I believed was right."

Craig smiled and gently patted him on the shoulder. I stood there in shock. Words. Pithy statements. To me they were all pointing in one direction, issuing the same mandate. First, there was the stranger who had been shot in front of me. Then Link. Weren't they both fighting for something they believed in, willing to make a heroic sacrifice for what they thought was the right thing? Wasn't I doing the same? Was it possible that even Jimbo had been driven by the same inclination?

Craig and I gazed at our battered friend and wondered if he could survive. The doctors gave his mother a rather optimistic prognosis. Their opinion was that whoever had given him the beating were pros; they knew how to put a hurt on a person but not permanently impair him.

The physicians were correct. Link made discernible progress and would, in a very short period of time, return to work. Neither Craig nor I ever heard him speak again about his movement. He did continue to write music. He also performed a special service for me not too long after his mishap.

CHAPTER 14: HAPPY TIMES

My home had been transformed in a matter of a few weeks. Everything I'd wished for my family, they had. Jewel insisted on working as much as she could, but Garland continually pestered her that her job was to stay home and raise the children. Money? No shortage now that Garland had made a quasi-move-in. He was loaded to begin with, and on top of that, he was taking in even larger amounts of cash from the fresh crop of rappers and rhythm and blues artists coming to his shop.

"Spend. Spend. Spend." Garland would encourage—entreat—Jewel. The man sounded like a past president. He wasn't suggesting; he was begging. "Spend. Spend. Spend." he'd hound Jewel almost daily.

On this particular afternoon, Jewel had taken Shana shopping for clothes. By the time they arrived back home, the sun was setting. Both ladies were carrying bags filled with purchases. Jewel looked haggard from a rough workout of spending on the children, but Shana was fluttering, her normal force of energy driving her body movement. Shana looked like a hip, trendy teen, while Jewel remained beautiful in her standard common dress.

When they walked in, Garland was sitting in front of the television but rose to greet them. He circled around the ladies slowly, surveying the girls like two fillies from his stable of fine ponies. He gave both of them a kiss on the cheek. As always, he seemed delighted.

"Shop at Vermillion's and this is how you come home, little lady," he commented to Shana.

"You seem especially chipper, Garland," Jewel addressed him in a patronizing manner.

"Jewel, darlin', when am I not?"

"You never get in bad moods, do you?" Shana posed, as if working on a puzzle.

"That's how I keep from having to get out of them," he whooped.

"Garland," Shana addressed him with her admonishing adult tone, "humans can't help being in a bad mood sometimes, 'cause bad things happen. People who can't let themselves feel bad get their feelings all jumbled up. When they should be sad, they're not; and they're happy for the wrong reasons." Shana looked gravely at a man she was treating like a clinical patient. "Now Garland,

181

what happens is they're so confused about feelings they're afraid to be in close relationships. So, the question is what to do. There are a number of theories…"

"I'm just a happy cat," Garland chirped at the precise moment he saw Dion enter the room. "And tonight I'm going to teach your brother how to be happy too."

"You buying me a car," Dion grumped at the suggestion that Garland might teach him something, especially how to achieve a state of joy—he hadn't experienced a feeling close to pleasure since I left.

His comment about the car roiled Jewel. She launched an evil eye toward her son to silence his disrespect.

"I've got a surprise for you, Mr. Dion," Garland smiled hugely. "Indeed, I do have a big one. It's so big you couldn't find it in a Ferrari dealership."

He was proud of his wit but Dion saw no humor.

"What?" Dion answered crankily, discharging him as a joker.

"Oh, nothing much…just signed a new client."

"Garland, you have them all, don't you?"

"Dion, if I don't take what the world is offering, someone else will. Someday you'll understand. It's not greed for more money. After all, how much can a person spend?" he proudly posed. "You know what drives me, Dion?"

"Power? I guess that's it."

"That's right. But for me it's a special type of power. I like to know that anyone I deal with, I can destroy. A man who fears you might want to kill you but will never try."

"Garland, you're saying all you do is destroy people?" Dion commented nonplussed. "Man, that's dark."

"Ha, ha! Not dark for me. And so you'll not be mistaken, that's not all I do. If you listened carefully, you'd have heard me say, 'I like to know that anyone I deal with I can destroy.' Why would I destroy them when they're making me money?" Garland exulted.

"And what about the people you can't destroy? You can't ruin the life of a president," Dion cleverly asserted.

"Dion, stay away from people you can't have power over—that's my advice on that matter."

Jewel took offense to Garland's attitude. Dropkicking a question, she aimed somewhere below his waist.

"Do you suppose you can destroy me?"

She was asking herself the question more than Garland. It had never dawned on her that that might be exactly what he was doing, not because he intended it but because of the fact that he could never feel secure otherwise.

"You're not business, baby. That's a whole different thing," he swooned, but with a whiny tone.

Jewel backed away from the subject, knowing it was futile to try and take it further. Garland had no interest in pursuing a conversation that was potentially contentious. Besides, he had something more pleasant in mind.

"So Dion, care to guess who the new man is on

Garland's list of top artists?" he glistened, proceeding without waiting for an answer. "You may know him… Angel Face."

"Angel Face…you?" Dion commented incredulously. "You signed…"

"Angel Face. How do you like that one? Little Shana, want to meet him?"

The girl was speechless, her silence a rare event.

"Landed a big one kids, huh? A whale. But that's the beginning. It just so happens that he's coming here soon to toast to a bright future with the one and only," Garland announced while gloriously pointing his finger at the heart of The Great One.

"Here…tonight?" Dion couldn't believe he might meet the hip-hop artist that he considered his idol. "Sure!"

"Would I lie?"

"Yeah," both Dion and Shana answered in perfect harmony.

"He's a famous rapper, man," Dion said, waving to Garland as if he finally understood the tease. He turned to walk away. "Give me a break."

When the doorbell rang, Garland noticed Shana rushing to get it, but he signaled for her to stop.

"Why don't you get it, Dion? Go see for yourself."

Lackadaisically, Dion walked to the door, still believing he was going to be made the brunt of a gag. But when he opened it…there was Angel Face. Dion looked the part of a young boy who had been kissed for the first time by a girl.

"You must be Dion," Angel smiled. As he glanced across the room, he took notice of an equally over-whelmed young girl. He'd already been schooled on their names. "And you're Shana? Hey there, Ms. Jewel."

Both Shana and Dion nodded to Garland, paying due respect for the unimaginable experience.

"So," Angel Face addressed both Dion and Shana, "let's see…what are you both thinking of doing now that you have Angel Face in your house?"

"Whatever you want to do," a star-struck Dion mumbled.

"Yeah, whatever you want," Shana dittoed her brother.

Angel flipped an iPhone out of his coat pocket, flashing it like a gold checkbook.

"Well kids, I wanna listen to some tunes."

"I know you're going to get a Grammy this year. I just know it's your time," Dion gushed.

"I'm glad you're sure," Angel said humbly.

"Wouldn't even be close."

"Dion, I like you already, buddy."

"You know, Angel, Dion's a bit of a performer himself," Jewel piped in.

"Oh, is that right?"

"Yeah," interjected Shana, "he wants to be the next you."

"Shut it, Shana." Hushing her, Dion addressed Angel. "I perform a little. I'm doing a concert at my school."

"Start small, end big," Angel advised.

"That's the plan."

"And don't give up. Shana, isn't that right?"

"I guess so," the little one answered Angel, still too taken by the moment to reclaim her mouthpiece.

"Well, who's gonna put this music on?" Angel asked, holding out his all-purpose device.

Garland took it and used the cable from the entertainment center to play it.

"So…show me what you got," Angel invited Dion.

"No way. I couldn't."

"I thought you wanted to make it big. Here's your shot. I know rappers who'd probably kill to show me what they got," Angel laughed. Then he addressed Shana. "You want me to start this off?"

No answer, but the girl concocted a bodily gyration fit for a contortionist as her face oozed an unrestrained grin.

"Let's do it," Angel yelled out as he began tapping his shoe on the floor. "What do you say we get into some "Real Feel Music"?

That was it for Shana. It was the song she hadn't been able to stop humming and singing for weeks. She was jumping up and down like a teen at a rock concert. She glanced at her mom.

"I feel that real feel music, yes I do," she sang, still

186

working her little body up and down as if she were preparing a launch from Cape Canaveral.

"All right then, let's do it," Angel instructed as the beat rose out of the speakers.

Angel Face had set the machine to play "Real Feel Music." The song was just that, the purest expression of real sound eliciting real feeling. The beat was fast, full of life, and insisted that the performers leave behind, at least for the time being, any sorrow or pain they were living through.

All five had lines to sing. The whole group handled the ensemble: "Come now, get some real feel music, bum around to some real feel music, come now, get some real feel music in your life, it feels so right."

Angel began with his solo. "You know that real feel music, I tried it for size and it fit like a woman in a lovin' man's eyes. Took a little listen and it tingled inside, for the first time, I had butterflies. It's that simple when you got a smooth lick, a bumpin' bass line and some drums that kick, a little bit of Ella, some Snoop or some Big, whatever be the recipe that you gonna dig. It kinda makes the world get moved and it holds us together while we bond and fuse, musicians dream for the tune and then we dream we can share it with you."

Angel was dancing around the room, jazzed on a tune he had written. Still, he was ready to bring in the recruits. "I won't cry now, but it's making my eyes wet, and I'm alive now without a single regret. So I'll give it to my man Dion, you know the words, go ahead, sing on."

Dion was in gear, ready for takeoff. "Well I wrote a bit of music and it sticks like a stamp, I wet it with my tongue, but where will it land? If I could jump to the rooftop, I'd flip a little lovin' to the people I saw, I think I'd get a tiny mic stand, put the mic in my hand so I could it kick down to all of my fans. All I want to do in this world of abuse is get funky, kick it, and make you feel loose. So play with me in this symphonic groove, and rock with me until you feel it too."

Angel didn't need to prompt Shana. "I want to get some singing time too, just a little bit before the good time is through. It's my turn, so you better stay, just as I tell you, just as I say. Get a little loose like me, 'cause we gonna dance and we gonna party. By the time I've done my part, you're gonna love me from the core of your heart. I feel this real feel music too, yes I do."

They "bummed" around with the real feel chorus until their lungs fatigued. Then with the music playing in the background, Dion and Shana took Angel Face to the far end of the room—so Shana could gape at him and Dion could get tips for his career. Garland led Jewel to the dining room where they could be alone.

"Garland, thanks. Dion needed that."

"I never met a better kid," Garland complimented.

"I'm sure you have. Since all this happened, he's been hurting. He's got all sorts of problems. Grades are slipping. All of a sudden, the school called and said he's been getting into fights. He was even suspended for the first time," Jewel said with exasperation. "He's never been like this."

"We all had our share of brawls growing up," Garland laughed.

"It's not just Dion. Dion is not being Dion, that's for sure. But it's Shana too; Shana's not being Shana. They're both mouthy and disrespectful from out of the blue. You see it," she asserted, imploring him for agreement—but he said nothing. "I'm trying to be understanding and patient, but I feel like smacking those faces."

"She's growing up, Jewel. What little girl doesn't get fresh with their mom from time to time?"

"Garland, I'm trying to talk to you," she said forcefully and with notable irritation.

Jewel was staring with a queer expression, awed by Garland's superficiality. Again the doorbell rang. Jewel stood to answer it. As she did, Garland went into the living room to talk with Angel and the children. It was turning into a busy evening in the Wright home.

Georgia rushed in. She was winded and flighty.

"Honey." She took a deep breath before proceeding with her briskly paced babble. "I'm a hop and jump out of the front seat with a bottle of somethin' strong and an inchin' for somethin' wrong from leavin' those children."

"Children!? You don't…"

"No, no, darling. That's for another time."

189

Georgia paused and scanned the room, noticing all the packages still spread on the floor.

"Wow. I'll give ya a thousand a piece for them two right there." She gazed again at all the parcels. "You bought out the store today, my dear?"

"Children needed clothes. I wonder, though, is that supposed to make me happy?"

"Ouch! Let me try that again. Hi, I'm your friend, Georgia. That's a lovely bunch of whatever's in them fancy bags you got. You done well for yourself."

"Georgia, I just don't know what to do. I may be buying out stores but I can't buy myself half a grin, let alone a smile."

Jewel picked up a couple bags and dropped them on the couch, taking out the contents. Georgia assisted her as she inspected the various articles of clothing.

"You sound like what I sound like every Wednesday from six to seven in the evening in Dr. Rosenbaumberg-erstein's…whatever his name's office."

Jewel was unable to contain a giggle of amusement. The talent for bringing laughter out of her was one thing she'd always appreciated about Georgia. "So, what does he say?"

"That if I don't start straightening out my life, he's raising his fee," she chortled.

"That might be a cheap kick in the ass," Jewel chuckled, nearly matching her friend's humor.

"Yeah, well, I can find a man to kick mine any time… for free."

Jewel noticed as she glanced across the room that Garland was grooving to the music, happy as a lark.

"Ever feel like you're wishin' for a good ass kickin' so you know for sure what's going on, just to feel something…if only for a moment?"

"Maybe. That's why I always keep a man on the side who can make a wishin' for a good ass kickin' come true."

"Georgia," Jewel addressed her friend with words laced half with tears and half with laughter, "I'll tell you, I always feel better after a couple minutes with you."

"Oh yeah? Well, honey, don't speak too soon 'cause you ain't gonna like this. I saw Mr. Benny Wright today," intentionally blathering my name, "and he didn't look good, no ma'am. He looked like a dirt rag with a…?

"Maybe that hussy of his dropped him," Jewel shot out bitterly.

"I don't know, I won't guess. I just had to tell you, that's all."

"I know," Jewel said sadly.

"Oh, my dear." Georgia embraced Jewel, trying to console her obvious grief. "You keep that precious chin of yours up. This is the worst part."

"Georgia, I wish I could be sure of that. I hate to admit it but I'm starting to think I'm no different than Benny."

"What are you talking about, girl?"

"Don't you think I look like a damn whore myself?"

Jewel whispered to her friend. "I've got a man basically boarding with me who will pay anything to get into my pants and I'm milking him. Jewel Wright, Biggest Sap, Class of 2012."

"You're being a bit too hard on yourself, love. Besides, Benny started this."

"Georgia, do you think it's possible to want something so badly that if you don't get it you become distraught enough to destroy everything you do have?" Jewel broke into sobbing. "It's tragic, just tragic. Everything ruined; no way back."

"I'm sorry, darlin'."

"No exceptions can be made for betrayal," Jewel harshly declared. Then she hugged her friend. "What could I do? I had to take care of those children. Benny and I said from the beginning of our family that we were going to better their lives. So, what's a little humiliation for every moment of the rest of my life?"

As Jewel finished the sentence, Garland joined them.

"Am I missing out on all the fun, girls?"

"Well, whoopee. Who do we have here? My boss. We'll let ya know if any fun starts, ya know, like if we get to plannin' to end someone's career or get to..." she smiled as she made clear to Garland she was quoting one of his famous sayings, "'make room for a big fish.' Isn't that the great stuff, honey, the stuff you wake up smilin' for every morning?"

"Am I that bad?" Garland moaned.

In harmony, both Jewel and Georgia had the answer, the one he'd have bet on. "Yep!"

"But, darlin', I don't judge," Georgia giggled. "God knows I've got no right for that."

"And I try not to. You've got your uses." Jewel, inspired by Georgia's comedic presence, managed to add playfully. "Come to think of it, you're all the fun I'd never ask for."

"Wonderful!" Garland swelled with excitement. "'Cause I've got an idea."

"What?" Jewel laughed.

Garland motioned for Jewel and Georgia to follow, taking them back to the living room. He yelled over to Dion and Shana, both still enamored with Angel. "Come over here for a minute. Dion. Shana. What do you think about a vacation?" he winked to Angel. "I'm thinking about a beach…somewhere say…in…I'm thinking about Hawaii."

"Hawaii?" Shana shouted in disbelief.

"Hawaii?" Dion plucked the word like a flat note.

Jewel stood expressionless next to Georgia.

"You'll love it, Dion. You're not too young for the ladies, are you?"

Shana was in a double trance—Angel, and now Hawaii. She'd regained her verbose ways.

"This is going to be great," she exalted, her vibrancy commanding everyone in the room to listen. "Did you know that actually there are 132 islands, extending over 1,500 miles in the North Pacific Ocean?"

Recognizing what was about to happen—a long discourse on the history of the state—her audience lost interest. They all turned and went about their business, leaving Shana alone—but she never missed a beat.

"Almost all of the people live on just seven of the islands and most of those are on Oahu. Captain Cook discovered these beautiful islands in 1778. The big island of Hawaii has Mauna Kea, the famous mountain…"

A faint impulse must have tickled her on the side of her tummy, her most sensitive spot. She paused to scratch what she thought was an itch, but in so doing, noticed that in fact, instead of an itchy feeling, she had sensed the movement of everybody in the room, all having abandoned her. Slowly, she peeked around, verifying that she was indeed alone. She smiled and envisioned herself a famous actress on stage.

"Okay," she yelled out so that everyone in the room had to hear. "I'll explain it all on our way there…on the plane."

On the surface, the Wright family might have seemed all fun and games, mingling with a celebrity, going on shopping sprees, and planning trips to Hawaii. But about the same time the residents were dancing and singing to "Real Feel Music," I was making a sharp plunge into a world of hell. Simon's premise that permitting myself to fully experience my emotions would strengthen me was proving to be false. Ironically, the more I felt, the weaker was my capacity to cope. Simon was killing me with kindness, and I wondered if he might be the devil in disguise sent to punish me once and for all.

I believe I heard something about "a dirty rag" and "Benny Wright not looking good?" It was true. The junkie in me who'd previously gloated over my brilliance for having orchestrated perfection beyond my own imagination had recently begun overdosing on street-hurt.

It was a gradual process; insidiously, my heart began to ache uncontrollably. I played dumb, proclaiming I couldn't account for the suffering. But I knew deep in my unconscious that only a short period had passed, yet I had been sentenced to life without the possibility of parole—could I survive or would I end up dying for having done the right thing?

CHAPTER 15: SHARP TURNS

I arrived at Jimbo's one morning just in time to meet the owner as he was unlocking the joint. I was the only customer, but since it was a Saturday I assumed it wouldn't be long before I'd be joined by some of the other regulars. I was sitting on a bar stool with a soft drink in front of me when Craig ran in the door.

"Been looking all over for you," he called breathlessly. "I never imagined you'd be here...eleven in the morning? You are going down fast, son."

"It's just a soda," I laughed, forcing a response that suggested happiness.

"I'm worried for you. All of a sudden you've been missing shifts at work—they can fire you for job abandonment," my friend warned.

"Don't worry, buddy, it's only been the last week or so," I responded indifferently.

"It seems like you're avoiding me, Benny. What's going on?" Craig questioned sympathetically.

"You're getting it all wrong. I'm great."

I wasn't willing to give up the pretense of confidence with anyone other than Simon, with whom I was more frequently expressing doubt as well as sharing my despondent mood. "Keep your head up; it has to get better," was the motto I kept trying to peddle.

Craig went to the heart of the matter. He insisted that I had deluded myself into accepting as a gem dropped from the sky the fortuity of Jewel and Garland hooking up; the relationship between my wife and Garland was a fact that Craig had brought to my attention earlier, but my friend was unable to move past his shock and appall.

"So tell me, buddy, have you seen Jewel and the children...I mean since...? Craig asked tentatively.

"Yeah. I told you it was going to work out perfectly, didn't I?"

"Are you telling me this was all part of your grand plan...?"

"Craig, didn't I tell you it was...The Perfect Plan?"

"Garland, a Perfect Plan?" Craig leaned forward and slumped his head over, in a gesture of total disbelief.

"Garland has wanted her since he set eyes on her in grade school. You know that. No, I didn't think it would be Garland, but it makes perfect sense. Hell, it didn't take long for him to..."

"Get out of here, kid. There's nothin' perfect about a good friend and a man's wife…"

"Oh, stop right there," I instructed. "For me, everything about a good friend and a wife is perfect. I didn't understand it until it happened, but Garland was like the last number that needed to tumble into place to open the safe. Like I pledged, the plan, it was…guaranteed."

"But it's not right for her," Craig vehemently protested.

"He's right for *them*! When you have a family of your own, you'll know that what I've done is nothing but right," I convincingly corrected my friend.

"Well then, my God, Benny. I'd call you a genius if it didn't look like hell just came crashing down on you."

"I'm in heaven man. Heaven just ain't always how it seems," I argued, leaking out a sign of the pain that begged for a shoulder to lean on.

"Well, I hope my heaven's a hell of a lot better than yours."

Craig was looking at me. He seemed concerned. I didn't understand how pathetic I appeared.

"You're hurting, Benny. I can see that. I'm worried it's going to break you," Craig expressed gravely.

"Break? Me? Benny Wright? Ha." I paused and looked at the sorrow in my friend's face. "You may have a point there…but I'll go down…knowing I fought for what I believed was right," I proclaimed like a punch-drunk zealot.

"Don't go down at all. I care for you, Benny. Friends like you don't come around that often."

I used all my might to smear my face with a smile before I left Craig. By later that day, I was in full grin again, successful in retaining that same dumb look on my mug when I passed a shop on my way to…wherever I was headed next. It wouldn't be long before my face would be more permanently wiped clean of its last crumbs of cheer. It was my own damn fault.

Simon was aware of my plan, but ironically, I'd failed to tell him about the murdered man. I believe it was just prior to that visit to Jimbo's, and my conversation with Craig about Garland being with Jewel, when I finally brought it up to him.

"What do you think about this mysterious man I met under the most improbable condition?" I posed to him after recounting the evening of the murder.

"Probably a junkie or petty drug dealer who betrayed his supplier."

"So, you don't believe he was there for a purpose?"

Simon bellowed. He wasn't mocking me. Rather, my question highlighted to him a principle of universal folly he found sadly hilarious.

"Benny, life seems to me to be made up of billions and billions of logical and rational events. They're actually random circumstances but they make up real history, each of our personal pasts and the record of mankind in general…and we largely ignore them. Then there's a tiny, miniscule fraction of happenings that are seemingly, unimaginably improbable, so remotely unlikely to occur that we deem them decreed by a higher power. These oddities we classify as mystical or magical.

"Ah, but they're the ones we spend time dwelling on. Heck, the lousy few of them are so powerful they dictate more than anything the thrusts, currents, waves, and patterns of man's behavior. From those scattered statistical infrequencies—events actually highly plausible because the unlikely becomes increasingly more probable as time passes—philosophies and theologies are born, with civilizations and cultures sustained on their backs and destroyed in turn when trampled on by the same folly. Hell, man created gods for the sole purpose of asking protection from those disempowering and terrifying experiences."

"Yes, but what if these few are in truth ordered by a divine authority?" I wondered out loud. "What if they are a rarity because He doesn't want to make His presence obvious?"

"Then you can believe that and guide your life by whimsical instruction."

"It seems that's how I created the mess I'm in," I admitted.

"One time, Benny. We'll see if you choose to repeat this type of behavior to a pattern."

"I might have made more of the encounter with the man than I should have?" I meekly entertained.

"I believe recently you mentioned the word 'desperation.'" Simon chirped. "It's from that state of mind that man invented all of the religions throughout history. Can't see where he's ever been able to break the habit. Can you?"

I shook my head, not even sure the gesture was in response to his query.

"We're not talking about faith," Simon added. "That's a different topic."

Maybe Simon was right. In my shattered and hopeless condition, arriving back from New York, I had ascribed to the dying man divine providence. More likely, he was no more than Simon surmised, a sad drug addict or dope peddler—still, that didn't warrant dropping the faith I held in my soul.

*****

After the discussion I had with Craig, I left Jimbo's. I recall stopping off at another saloon to drink through the hurt I concealed from him. The alcohol must have succeeded to temporarily sooth my woes, because I had absolutely no recollection of anything that transpired from shortly after taking the first sip of liquor until at some point when I found my way home and fell asleep.

I know there was this gap of unaccounted time because when I awoke it was an unpleasant reentry into my conscious life. I was drenched in the tears of an agonizing sleep experience. The locale for my hideous dream was Jimbo's. In that sleep-state, I was with Craig, just as I'd been in reality the previous day. In my illusory condition of sleep, I remember feeling listless. The imagery of the dream included me reaching under Jimbo's counter to pick up a guitar and starting to play a few notes. I had no inspiration for music and let gravity take the instrument lifelessly to the ground.

The best I can describe for what I experienced was the feeling of being otherworldly. I dropped my limp body into a chair. My eyes felt like the weight of lead and insisted on closing. There was total blackness in my mind. But then, after a few moments, a spotlight lit up what appeared to be half of a stage. There were Dion and Shana playing by the seaside on a pure white sandy beach. Behind them on a lounge, limp like a wildflower drooping wearily over a branch, was Jewel. She looked sad, but the scene had all the props set for joy; they were each in bathing suits, the sun was shining, the sea rolled as soft as a pillow, and all around were vague figures of people running and jumping on the sand and floating in the water.

I had a sensation of distance, as if I were thousands of millions of light years from the seaside scene, though I couldn't estimate what amount of space was in truth separating me from them. As I lay back, trying to follow the movement of my clan, I began to hear sounds. At first, I noticed the collective voices of all the people at the beach shouting and laughing, but then music began to play. I recognized the melody and the beat as one of my own, but the words were not ones I had written. As I listened, a voice I recognized as Jewel's began to sing.

When she finished her verses, the spotlight shifted to me. I was now also on a beach, hazily wondering how I got there. It was a black sand variety. There was nobody with me; my shoreline was dreary and desolate. The glaring light hit me like a hot prod and I bolted upward. I looked around. I thought I'd suffered a stroke. The world was a mystery. I was lost in a vast stretch of nothingness. I knew Jewel was there. Somewhere, I imagined, on the other side of the beach, on the other side of the light, on the other side of nowhere, but I couldn't see her. Still, when she finished her verses, I followed her with my portion of the song that I named, "Whose Life."

"Whose life did I buy?" Jewel mournfully posed. "I want to get used to a living with passion and rhyme, a living that's mine, oh I want a moment where loneliness dies. I'm losing feel and I'm losing sight, of all the feelings that kept me wrapped tight. My grip is light, stripped down on a beach white. Things seemed perfect to me, set in the sun like a fantasy, two children at play, laughing at laughter, without a cloud of gray. But this life doesn't feel like mine, so I cry on the sideline." Over and over she repeated the next two lines. "Whose life am I givin' a try? Doesn't feel like mine even when I cry."

I jumped into her performance. "I'm doing time and it's not even mine, drinkin' liquor in the day 'cause I can't write a rhyme. My eyes closed shut but I can't see, blind to the world where I used to live. Fantasy, may be life's greatest gift, up in the clouds I could smile while I sit. I thought I had it all set in stone, divine inspiration had given me gold, lifted me up like a king to his throne to watch as my kingdom thrives a happy home. But, I left myself all alone; this doesn't feel like home" Then I repeated the same lines as Jewel. "Whose life am I givin' a try? Doesn't feel like mine even when I cry"

Following verse was prose; we were speaking sentences that made it appear as if she and I were engaged in conversation, exchanging thoughts. "I want to get anxious to lie in bed," she sadly shared as I countered with, "I want to lay a kiss on my little kid's head." "I want to walk in shoes that don't shine," Jewel said painfully. "Why's it hurt when I know I did fine?" I admitted. "Something feels off today," she panted. "Nothing went wrong I can honestly say," I followed. "I'm lost in a house so big," Jewel despaired. I ended with a dinger. "But I'm losing it, losing it."

It was like a miracle because during the moments we were alternately sharing our sentiments, her voice seemed to be coming from every direction at once and at the same time from no place. I wasn't able to locate Jewel in space. But as we shared each line, I noticed that we came into ever more perfect unity. Then, just when we were about to start the chorus again…I saw her.

She was sitting in the same pose as when I first

noticed her on the beach. Now she was crying. As I watched her, I realized that I was teary too. At the exact same second, she and I each took an identical white handkerchief out of our pockets. Synchronized, we dabbed our left eye first and then the right. We were in immaculate harmony.

Each of us stood up straight, tilted our heads at precise forty-five-degree angles to look up at the sky, paused, and then closed our eyes at the same instant. I watched every detail from the darkness of my dream state. Jewel and I, we were the same, a perfect one; but we couldn't touch one another.

The scene then turned to a prison. I remember that we were both inside and outside the steel bars at the same time, trying to get to the other side of anywhere, together yet separate. Of course, in dreams everything is distorted. The sketching in this case painted a picture of horror. We both started screeching as loudly as we could, the sound finally bursting me out of the dream and into hell.

I woke still screaming but with nobody to hear me other than the four alien walls of the real cell where I was living.

It was not only the horror of the sound I was producing. I ejected out of the dream like a jet fighter pilot abandoning his craft after being hit by a missile. My head nearly hit the ceiling as I transitioned from dream to being awake. What I saw and heard as I relived the dream, devastated me. I lay in bed, the obvious dream wish of Jewel and me to hook up with one another countermanded by the recognition that for weeks she'd not made any attempt to contact me, even to express her rancor for my refusal to send money.

I never fell back to sleep, yet I had no shortage of energy for the day. I was running on a battery fully charged with fear, dread, and pity. I didn't want to die, but I didn't know if I had the courage to go on living either.

CHAPTER 16: I WAS WRONG ALL THE WAY

The dream I had about Jewel and the children at the beach no doubt was preceded by a period of several hours—still, I couldn't recall what happened to me for that entire span of time. I assumed a portion was spent sleeping, but even so, there was a healthy interval that was entirely lost to consciousness; most notably where I had been from the time I left Craig and went to the other bar until I eventually fell asleep.

When I was able to examine it some weeks later from a more objective perspective, a vague association came to mind, a condition of the psyche I remembered reading about in a college psychology class—a fugue state. One afternoon I mentioned it to Simon. He didn't comment when I first brought it up, but the next day when I saw him he smiled devilishly.

"I decided to do some research on fugue states."

"You didn't have to do that," I told him.

"I was curious. Besides, it may have cured my twitch about becoming a psychologist."

"How is that?"

"Have you ever seen the book the mental health profession uses to diagnose people?"

"I have no idea it exists."

"It's called the *DSM Manual of the American Psychiatric Association*," he enlightened me as he passed a copy for my inspection.

It was thick. I was astonished as I browsed it, that there were hundreds of pages.

"My Lord, Simon. Would I be irreverent if I called this a terrifying little volume?"

"Not at all. The only compliment I can deliver is that I concluded these guys and gals in the profession are equal opportunity docs. They invented labels to cover just about every imaginable mental, psychological, emotional, and behavioral state a human can experience—and deemed them 'disorders.' Frankly, I doubt that saints, angels, and even gods could escape without being tagged abnormal."

"They'd have a ball with me."

"Benny, they'd have a field day with Gods."

"I bet," I concurred, still scanning the pages.

"It's no joke," Simon chuckled. "If Zeus stepped into the office of a modern-day psychiatrist he'd leave weeping. God help him—and Zeus was the supreme ruler of all the Greek gods. Did you know he had a weapon he used to punish anyone who displeased him, a mean thunderbolt he could employ to sizzle a gang of wise guys faster than an alcoholic can break a vow of sobriety. There's more that a clinical analyst would drool over. He was married to Hera, yet he was famous for many affairs. Still, he had the gall to use his fireball on those who lied or broke oaths. Sounds like a sociopathic personality?"

"Seems like it," I answered perfunctorily.

"His wife, Hera, would be in hopeless trouble too—not surprising, living with a madman like Zeus. She was his wife while doubling as his sister. Multiple personality? And Aphrodite? Her magical power to compel anyone she wished to desire her, her greedy appetite for making love would definitely earn her a sexual disorder. Hades? What's to say? The dude grabbed up all the dead he could and wouldn't let go of any of them—talk about greed...and necrophilia. Plus, he had rotten socialization skills."

I paused to give thanks. I was in fairly good shape after all. The most I could be accused of was a single, short-lived episode of a dissociative disorder. In my case, exactly as diagnosed—after consulting with the American Psychiatric Association Diagnostic Manual—a fugue state.

"I'm celebrating, Simon. Listen to this. A fugue state is defined as lasting from a few hours to days during which time the individual engages in unplanned travel or wandering—for me there was no establishment of a new identity, which can occur during this adventure into amnesia."

"Exactly as I read it, Benny. You were let off light by the psycho wizards...this time," he teased. "God only knows, it could have gone a lot worse," he giggled.

The following morning, I discovered the mystery of what had occurred during the blacked-out sojourn, subsequent to having awakened from the dream.

Here's how the awareness finally came to me. After I was able to dress and groom myself, I left my place. Then I wandered the streets aimlessly for a couple of hours, trying to sort out in my mind the events of the prior evening. Failing to do so, I had unconsciously gravitated away from my apartment, toward Jimbo's. When I arrived, I took a seat on a stool. I felt heaviness inside my whole being, as if the universe had imposed the entirety of its weight on me.

Jimbo looked at me, and without asking, slid a mug of coffee across the counter. A moment later, Craig walked in. Following behind was Link, limping, with his face still showing considerable bruising. He looked remarkably improved from how he'd appeared in the hospital— he definitely had amazing healing powers.

Mimicking Craig's words from the morning before, Link admonished, "Eleven in the morning, Benny."

"I told you, Link," Craig addressed his friend. "He's here all the time."

"Um. Um. Eleven in the morning," Link repeated.

"Yeah, eleven!" Craig emphasized.

"What's wrong with a little time *at peace* once in a while?" I countered dopily.

"Look at yourself," Craig cried out mournfully. "Benny, what's wrong? If I can help, you know I'll do anything. Hell, we all make mistakes."

"I'm trying to go backward in time, solve a riddle, that's all."

"We can tell that, Benny. We've been seeing you not looking so good for some time," Link added.

"I had a dream last night." I spoke as if I was still in a reverie. "It kept going on and on, seemed like all night."

"It wasn't all night, Benny, I can tell you that for certain," Craig said.

I went on in wonderment, never processing my friend's definitive statement. "It was like an old-time album with the needle stuck in the groove. It was so real it scared me."

Craig and Link looked curiously at one another, sadly shaking their heads to commiserate with my woeful state.

"The dream was about Jewel and the children. Wait! More is coming back to me. Jewel and I were singing to each other on a beach and then…it went blank…but… there was more singing, I think. It all seems out of order;

211

the way dreams get jumbled up? You guys remember the kid I sort of mentored, Die4U? He was there. I'm sure of it. I remember now. Yeah, he was wearing this silk maroon…I think it was the dream…I think so. Anyway, it was a tight-fitting shirt that was unbuttoned to the navel and he was also wearing black leather pants."

While I was describing the images in my mind, Craig and Link were again gazing at one another, this time befuddled.

"Oh, was Die4U there, Benny?" Link smirked, entreating me to continue. "Why don't you tell me more about this…dream?" Link looked with amazement a second time toward Craig, as he instructed me to go on with my story.

"All I can recall is having a terribly bad afternoon yesterday. I felt more alone than ever in my life. After I left you Craig, I went out to drink…did I come in here at some point?" I yelled over to Jimbo.

Surprisingly, Jimbo gestured I had not.

"Did I ever mention that when all this started, I happened to witness a man killed?" I asked them. Neither indicated that I had. "That's really not it, the murder itself. It was what the man said to me as he was dying. He drew me close to him, and I remember his words. Link, they were almost the same as what you said. I still hear that dying man as if he's telling to me: "Sometimes we have to do the right thing, even if we die…"

"So what do you make of that, Benny?" Craig asked.

212

"I'm not sure if he finished the sentence but…"

"Benny, the man was dying."

"I know, but hearing him, I realized what I had to do. Then Jimbo was talking about it being better for everybody after he was kicked out by his wife and Link later talked about fighting to the end if you believe in something; it all kept coming more and more in order."

"Terrific reasoning, friend. The man is dead. Link, with all due respect, had the living daylights beat out of him and is barely in one piece. Jimbo lost his whole family."

"Well, it all made sense at the time."

"So…what about the dream?" Craig queried, a rare occasion when he seemed impatient with my perceived nonsense.

"I went out last night but I can't recall a thing I did. I have no idea where I was or if I was with anyone. Whatever I did and whatever happened, I know I woke this morning from the dream about Jewel and me singing on the beach. Craig, I'm freaking out about something and I can't put my finger on it."

"Because of this dream?" Craig asked excitedly. "You're saying the dream is freaking you out."

"It's everything, each element of the reality I'm seeing in my head now; that's what's scaring me. It's too vivid. Die4U was dressed like a star. He was standing on stage. Then, when he looked out at the audience and saw me, he stopped. He smiled at me and then said…"

213

Link filled in Die4U's next lines, beating me to it. "This is a special night for me. We all have someone that's been a special inspiration to our life; a mentor… mine is in the front row. Magic, come up and share a song with me."

I looked at Link with astonishment.

"Yeah, that's right," I grimaced. "Then he grabbed my arm and lifted me on stage…I felt like a feather…my body was weightless and I had no power to resist."

"You looked like you weighed closer to a ton of cement," Link laughed.

"At that moment," I continued, falling deeper into a spell, "I looked out into the audience…and I saw three broken hearts. The last three hearts I'd ever want to see busted. The three hearts I thought I was strengthening until that day…and Die4U started singing, and the music, it got real loud."

I lifted myself from my stool and looked outward beyond Craig and Link, both eagerly waiting for me to continue. Instead of seeing the walls and fixtures of Jimbo's, I noticed that I was blinded. Still, I kept talking to my friends.

"That's when the lights in my dream turned dim. I was still seeing those three broken hearts. They looked like florescent figures in the dark. I saw Jewel. She had that glow around her. It was the strangest thing because our eyes were the same eyes and at the same time they were looking at both of us.

214

"This is when the music became a distinct beat. I heard drums pounding like those three hurting hearts and a keyboard crying their tears. Those six heavy eyes, as piercing as a laser beam, locked on mine—they shot me full of holes. My senses turned to a metallic heaviness. I wanted to cry. I tried to scream out, but I couldn't speak.

"Then the microphone was in my hand. When I looked at it, I knew my power of vocalization had been restored. I was dreamy, feeling a world apart from everyone in the club where the event took place. The words I was singing spoke a truth that I knew all along but hadn't permitted myself to own, words that turned to whips used by each of the three broken hearts in the audience to lash me for my errant behavior—"I Was Wrong All The Way."

I imagined while explaining the dream to Craig and Link that I was hearing the same music. Spontaneously, I began repeating the lyrics, though I couldn't explain at that second where in my consciousness they were stored.

"How do I describe it, what do I feel, right before my eyes, but past a shield, my life, broken and peeled, and I'm culled from it so I can't help it heal. Six weeping eyes wasn't part of my plan, I kept looking back 'cause I couldn't have ran. It was intoxicating, and I can't understand, what went wrong with my clan."

In disbelief at the monstrousness of what I'd created, I continued. "I knew I was right, but I know I was stunned. I knew I was right, but I must have been dumbed. I knew I was right, 'cause God had just come, and put every answer on the tip of my tongue. I knew I was right, now I know I was off. I knew I was right, but I'm surrounded with loss. I knew I was right, but I was high on sauce, in the streetlight on a weeknight 'cause life lost cause."

By this time, I was talking the words and trying to digest the folly of my ways and the unimaginable consequence of what had seemed indisputably guaranteed.

"I knew I could help them if I could just leave, and with a bit of money they'd find some peace. I knew they'd move up, right through the ranks, to a life a luxury that I couldn't bank. And they moved up, it worked like a charm, lounging on the beach with palms, travelin' like kings from a castle, with help for any hassle. The plan went through…an hour ago I was right and I knew, but I saw something scary on the face of all three, they got what I wanted and they didn't need.

"Somehow, someway, somethin' went astray, and I'm out now, left only to pray. What am I to do now? Conceive a solution that's sound? No, I'm gonna sit this one out, and hope while I pray that things turn around. Cause that's the best I can be, silent, waiting, wishing." The truth had me drenched in tears by the time I was wrapping up the song. "I knew I was right, but I was high on sauce, in the streetlight on a weeknight 'cause life lost cause."

Honestly, if I could have put feelings to what I was experiencing, I'd say it was a total loss of sensation—a state of near collapse. I believed that the song I had just sung at Jimbo's was the one I'd had in my dream and that it must have preceded the one with Jewel on the beach. As I came out of the trance and sat back down, Craig and Link blasted my already confused mind into a worse state of chaos.

"Benny, you were there," Craig remarked.

"You were there," Link confirmed.

"Benny, it was real," Craig assured me.

"It was real?" I questioned bewilderedly.

"The only person in that place that looked worse than you…was Jewel," Craig reported.

I knew they'd never lie to me. I know now that what I've described happened at a concert that took place during the hours I couldn't remember—and what precipitated the real dream I had later when I imagined Jewel and me on the beach.

While I was singing "I Was Wrong All The Way," Jimbo had been in the back taking a delivery. He never heard a word we were speaking nor the song I performed. He assumed when he came in that I was bummed out over my grand plan failing. He wanted to cheer me up.

"Benny, come over here and give me a hand while we watch the next World Series winner, the Detroit Tigers."

"I'll pass, Jimbo."

"Cheer up, man," he advised, "you could have been

217

married to my wife. You got that Perfect Plan; you'll be fine."

"I need a new plan."

"Um, um. Just give it time. All things need time," Jimbo advised. He then permitted himself further commentary on my personality. "You give up too easily."

I couldn't help but laugh, though humor was the last emotion I was fit for. Jimbo couldn't have been more wrong again—my problem was not giving up but stupidly persisting where people with better judgment would have quit long before.

By this time, a few of the boys had come in and taken seats. But right after Jimbo and I spoke, the door opened and all action ceased, as if the joint were flash frozen.

It was Cookie, striding in like an actress waltzing across a stage.

"Hi, Benny," she said, as she stood next to her man. "Can I sit with you?"

"Sit with me, Cookie," Link clowned. "I can make you crumble."

Craig, more sensitive to my delicate state, had his own request. "Not now, Cookie. Not a good time."

I hadn't seen Cookie for quite a while. I also hadn't called to explain why I stopped taking her out. Cookie didn't come for an apology, excuse, or explanation.

"Oh, yes, Cookie," I responded, dismissing Craig's attempt to protect me. I motioned to a table where we could talk.

"Been thinking about you," Cookie said before we were seated.

"Yeah? I think about you too."

"A girl like me never had a chance, did she?"

Wearily, I looked up at her.

"We went to parties, we saw movies, walked at Belle Isle, clutching hands until they were sore, we sang tunes, played music...we paraded around the city and then... well, you know it all."

"You hate me too," I said mournfully, cupping my hands as a prop to rest my chin.

"No, Benny, you're one of the good ones. You're the type a woman can love."

"Don't say that. No. Love Benny; get hurt by Benny. And Heaven forbid Benny loves you," I said to castigate myself. "I gave them everything I thought they wanted and everything they didn't need. All they ever wanted was . . . me."

"I could have told you that the last time we sat chattin' together," Cookie giggled. "Hell, I could have told you that the last time we sat chattin' in these same two seats...if I hadn't been such a dummy thinking I might be the woman to take her place."

"Maybe I didn't want to figure it out. Lovin' ain't an easy thing. Maybe I didn't want to handle it. But what replaces a father...a husband?"

"So what now, kid?"

"I'm not sure what now, Cookie. I feel like I'm about to die," I moaned.

"It's not that bad, believe me."

"It is that bad. If I could dream another dream it would be I'd get them back. But I wouldn't stand a chance. Oh, I'd fight to get them to take me...but...it's useless."

"Honey, all you did was put them on hold. Men like you come around once in a lifetime and Jewel..."

"Hates me, Cookie. Once she got it in her head about you and me...you don't know Jewel."

"I'm going to tell you exactly what to do," Cookie said confidently.

I knew what she was attempting...a pep talk. As she spoke, I became ever more doleful.

"Brighten up that face, Benny," one of the regulars called out from across the room.

"Looks to me like he's given up again," Jimbo added with a frustrated shake of the head.

"That's right. I see it," the man agreed.

"And I believe I gave you clear instructions about giving up in Jimbo's...it don't fly," Jimbo admonished me.

"Don't worry, boys," Cookie yelled like a high school cheerleader. "I'm taking care of it."

"How is that, little lady?" Jimbo asked.

"Yeah, how is that, little lady?" the rest of the patrons mimicked.

"'Cause I'm gonna show him the way."

"The way to what?" the group questioned in unison.

Cookie came prepared. She'd written a song especially for the occasion, taking her lyrics and recording them over one of my beats. From her purse, she produced her CD and tossed it to Jimbo.

"Let's get Cookie rolling," she smiled. "I'm going to teach Benny the way to get moved, I'm going to give him "The Recipe to Get Moved."

Immediately, I recognized the sounds that came shooting out of the speakers.

She'd used the same beat that was playing at Jimbo's the night after my disappointment in New York, "Get Moved." Her lyrics were wonderful. It touched me that she'd gone to the trouble to write them, plus I couldn't have imagined she'd have the depth and imagination to put it together. There was a lot beneath the surface of Cookie. I knew it but hadn't, in all fairness, appreciated it enough—not long after the song was completed, I was going to get an even larger bite of this amazing Cookie.

"I've got the recipe, boys."

Cookie was woman all the way, knowing what a man needs to atone to a lady when she's mean as a bull.

"You, need the recipe to get moved, and do what you pray to do. So listen and I'll give you what you need me to. It's quite the task, I'll agree, but I can give you the recipe. You'll change her mind with just a bit of grind. Write this down I'd recommend, 'cause she'll rebut 'til the bitter end. From every angle and bend, you'll prod and she'll defend.

221

"The first step doesn't take a pro, give her a holler, but just for show. She'll hang up I know, but the seed you plant is sure to grow. Then when the time's right, find a place she goes at night. Show up in style with a smile, but don't reunite. Say not a word, not a peep, just be seen, and retreat, then you'll be swooshin' through her head all week.

"Now you're movin' on the kill like a matador, with a shining sword and a bull that's sore. This my friend, this is when you make your score. A gesture, not too large, live in person, prepared and on guard, something special, to make her smile, and fight denial. She'll fall to you inside at least, and long for you while she sleeps. Her heart will pound a beat that's loud, and you'll stand proud.

"You'll be ready with all your lines, one then the next falling in rhyme. It's bound to work; the plan is sublime. It's true. This is the recipe to get moved, and do what you pray to do. I'll give you everything that you need me to. Benny, move, do it with me. Groove, right through it with me. Get moved, smile with me tonight."

Cookie was precious. She was all business. After the song, she bent down to hug me. Then she picked up her bag and prepared to walk out.

"You know what to do," were her parting words, ominously reminding me of the comment Simon had made some time ago when he said to me, 'What to do will come to you; you'll see.'"

Was it Simon who had sent Cookie as a messenger? I still hadn't learned to stop looking for divine instruction in randomness.

My reply to Cookie was not encouraging.

"I can't thank you enough, Cookie. It's a great approach, but I doubt I'll ever get a chance to try."

She smiled as if I was daffy. Still, as Cookie left, I was certain it was way too late for Jewel and me. My education about my wife's views on fidelity began long before we consummated our marriage. Once she locked a law in her head, there was as much chance of changing it as convincing a woman that there's no difference between a cubic zirconia and a real diamond. With all that said, I wanted to call her. I wanted to try—one time to see if by chance miracles can come true.

I took a deep breath, the type that pauses the functioning of every organ in your body, that silences sound, that eerily quells any perception of emotion, that focuses one's vision on a black hole someplace in your brain's grey matter—that's what it was like for me as I listened to the sound on the other end.

One ring. A second. Finally, a third ring. Then I heard her voice.

"Jewel, it's Benny," I said tentatively.

Her hanging up would have devastated me had I not so recently experienced devastation. So, like a minus times a minus, the potentially mortally wounding T.K.O. punch positively turned into an inspiration.

"Wrap things up; prepare to fight." "You have to fight for what you believe in even if you might die trying." "Sometimes you have to do the right thing even if you die…" "You'll all be better off."

Those were the phrases I heard, repeating over and over. They were the same messages I'd embraced all through this wild journey I'd embarked on, but now they were suggesting a completely different objective. I had to fight to the death to undo the madness I'd created, to remove the suffering I'd inflicted on the people I loved most. I had to try even if it did mean I'd die. If only I had a plan I believed to be, "guaranteed to succeed."

I did hear music. It was real this time, and I poured my heart out putting lyrics to it, denouncing the rejection of her slamming the phone. I titled the piece, "Gotta Get Wrapped Up." It wasn't half bad.

"Gotta get wrapped up. Gotta get wrapped up, so I look just right, packed in a package she can't deny. Wrapped up like a nice surprise, so the moment we meet, she'll wanna see inside. I'm what they need and they always did, and I'm the only thing I could always give. A happy harmony hummed through the house, and I was deaf to it, though it was so damn loud.

"She always knew what I was taking away, the fire inside me that warmed the day, the magic in my name, and all the lovely nights that we'd cuddle and lay. I wanted rubies like chunks of green, to lather her up like royalty. I wanted fancy shiny things 'cause that's what everyone says that a woman needs. I wanted Christmas trees in the middle of spring, so every time I'd come home I'd have gifts to bring. But I'd never need a Christmas tree, to give the gift of me."

It felt so right—I was just warming up. I had a story to tell. I was inspired to own up to every truth. "Now that I lost her trust, I can only get back if I get past her disgust. I gotta shine up and look brand new, so she knows what I did I can no longer do. And she sees I can mend what I bent, and put us together so it lasts forever. Only then I can give them me, and we'll be back, as a family."

The joy was flowing. I wanted so badly to do what I still knew could never happen, mend us. Still, I prayed in words. "Gotta get wrapped up so I look just right, packed in a package she can't deny, wrapped up like a nice surprise, so the moment we meet, she'll wanna see inside"

When I finished singing, I ran the words through my head a few more times. I was pacing around the place. Then I looked at my phone. What was the use right then? She'd just hung up on me. I had to take the battle to the trenches. Cookie had armed me. I had heard her words and needed to pack them up for future use.

I have to "grind" down her resistance. I contemplated my next moves. By placing the first call to her, I'd already tried the "holler" just for show, to "plant the seed." Now, I had to "show up in style with a smile" where she might be at night. No words. Just enough to get her head "swooshin." She's sure to be mad as a "bull," so my first

225

"gesture, not too large" has to be enough so she'll have to "fight denial." She'll fall…I hope. *Is the plan "bound to work, sublime?"*

I did the best I could to stuff down the hopelessness that kept creeping into my head, but it seemed accomplishing it was a bit too pricy for my confidence-starved, low-budget status. In fairness, what could I expect? As I looked back to the prior months and outlined my behavior toward her, I couldn't help but evaluate the situation from her perspective. It didn't look good.

The way I had treated her could best be summed up with words beginning with "rep"—reprehensible, repulsive, repugnant, repellent, and reproachful. That was enough to earn a lifetime of revilement. I wasn't certain that Cookie's recipe had the ingredients that were sufficient to remedy that lineup of offensive behavior.

Still, I saw no choice but to dedicate myself to that miniscule outside chance that Cookie had it right. During the next couple of weeks, I tried everything in my power to take a soft approach to introducing myself back into her life. Cookie's counsel couldn't have produced worse results.

I timed it to show up at the market one afternoon when Jewel went out shopping—she walked out of the store when she saw me. One evening, I dressed like a prince and walked past the yoga studio where she took classes; she looked sickened to see my face, then she turned and went back inside the building.

She was picking up Shana from an after-school acting class. I parked in the lot where she could see me. She glared me out of her vision. I also sent flowers—it didn't help my outlook when the floral shop called the next day and informed me that the party they attempted delivery to slammed the door. Her parting words were reported to me by the store, she shouted, "Tell him to go to Hell!"

I was running out of faith. Can you really die trying to do what you believe in?

Then, one afternoon I met with Simon and out of the blue, he gave me a green light, told me it was time to up the stakes, to put it all on the line. Hearing him jacked me up to the point that I managed to gain enough courage to call again. She wasn't home.

It was for the better that she wasn't. The time for a showdown had arrived. I decided to refuse another angry dismissal. The thought of betting the house oddly pumped me up and was like music to my ears. The sound rose in volume…and this time I spoke the lyrics.

"I gotta get wrapped up so I look just right, packed in a package she can't deny. I'm getting wrapped up like a nice surprise so the moment we meet…yes, she'll want to see inside."

Up and down went my emotions. The last words, "she'll want to see inside," and the realization that she'd never allow herself a chance to look, socked my spirits.

CHAPTER 17: DITTO THAT

I was blessed that during this most anguishing period of wondering if I could patch things back together, I had the support of loved ones. Simon was always there to encourage me, and Craig was especially devoted, regardless of the fact that I'd not kept him as close to the unfolding drama as I might have. I had no conscious reason for excluding him but after Simon suggested I intensify the battle, I called Craig to fill him in on what I was about to do.

"I'm going over there...now," my muffled voice informed Craig.

"Good luck. I'll keep my fingers crossed for you, for both of you."

"Thanks, Craig. I'll never forget how you've been there for me. I know I didn't share everything with you like I should have to my best friend but..."

"I understand about you and Cookie," he chuckled, answering the question I couldn't for myself, that I knew the Cookie affair upset him and I didn't want to keep confronting him with behavior on my part that I was aware was troubling to him.

"What is it you understand?"

"Just go. I'll call Cookie and see if she can't send some support vibes by special delivery."

I was in a hurry to meet my destiny, causing me to drop the discussion that otherwise I might have pursued. I had to get myself "wrapped up," ready to face the fury of Zeus' wife, Hera, a lady known for her vengeance against those mortals who crossed her.

I dressed myself fine. I bolted out the door. I noticed my vomit-lime colored Chevy waiting for me. It took me about thirty seconds to gun the engine and aim toward Jewel. I couldn't seem to construct a speech that made any sense. Amazingly, I auditioned hundreds in the span it took me to make a quick stop and then reach what I had once called my home. I tried to silence the awful reality—that regardless, I likely wouldn't be permitted to make an appeal.

As it happened, when I arrived, Jewel had company. Just minutes before, Georgia had made a surprise visit of her own. Jewel had been standing near the kitchen counter and was applying clear covering to her new orange nail polish. The front door swung open, startling Jewel. There was Georgia, dressed in a get-up of exotically wild colors and a matching outward zaniness. Georgia scanned the room, as if she were investigating a crime scene.

"What are you doing here?" Jewel inquired of her friend who typically would not have come over without calling first.

"You don't want me either," Georgia moped.

She then approached Jewel, picked up the bottle containing the orange polish, opened it, and began brushing over every other of her already marine-blue colored fingers.

"What's wrong?" Jewel asked her friend.

"What's always wrong? I can't never find a way to keep my love alive."

"You can't keep your love alive? Well," Jewel now mimicked Georgia's style of speech, "honey, my love ain't exactly hoppin' and jivin' either."

"They always love me, to the bitter end," she carried on, paying no mind to Jewel's comment.

"Puts you far ahead of the field."

"Well, not quite, darlin'. Time I come clean. How many times have I brought a man over to your home for a lovely evening?" Georgia queried.

"None, actually."

"Right. And how many times have I been married?"

"None."

"Not quite." Georgia now lifted her left hand and began counting fingers, then switched to the right one.

When she counted the first finger of the second hand she stopped. "Six...at last count...six times I've been married."

"Six times you've what?"

"Not really. See, I ain't never been de—vorced."

Jewel was used to wild antics and lots of surprises with her friend. The fact that she was such a different type than most of mankind endeared her to Jewel, along with the fact that Georgia would never betray a friend and could be counted on at times of crisis for compassion and genuine empathy. This time, she had Jewel spinning her head several rotations.

"Six marriages? Six marriages? No divorces? And your best friend never once knew about one? What in god's name, Georgia, are you talking about?"

"And I loved every one of them up to the day they died."

"What did you do, kill 'em?"

"No. I didn't have to kill 'em, daggum it. But I hate to say they didn't just die off on their own either."

"This time, friend...you are going into new territory. I'm begging you. Don't mess with my fragile little head."

"Let me explain. You hold off now making a judgment, okay, love? All of my husbands, just happened to be locked up, incarcerated and on death row."

Revealing the bizarre circumstances, she then took a hanky from her purse and started to dab the corners of her eyes. The tears then began to stream.

231

"And She-She is going away tomorrow," she bellowed sorrowfully.

Jewel stared at her loony buddy, more astonished then she'd ever been.

"Who?! She-She?"

"Don't let no name fool you. He was as much man as any I've had and I've had...well, quite a few."

"I'm...sorry. Will you be okay?" Jewel asked, not quite sure how to react.

In an unexpectedly brief amount of time, Georgia recomposed herself. "I always am, right? My friend taught me the trick, and once I gave it a try I just couldn't get enough. You have to be cut out for this sort of time-limited relationship," Georgia lectured. "Not every girl is."

"You're serious?"

"I never told you because I didn't know if you'd understand."

"Georgia, I don't. But if it works for you..."

"Oh, it works all right. I'm deathly serious about it. In fact, I'll tell you what. They were six of the best relationships of my life." Georgia excitedly offered an addendum. "I'm heading down to the hoosegow to pick me up number seven before She-She turns cold; that's just how he'd want it."

"Well, Georgia, call me old-fashioned," Jewel spurned, "but when all this is over, I'll still be looking for something a little more long-term."

"Oh, I know just what you want, darlin'."

Jewel shook her head, still not believing what Georgia had told her.

"Look," Georgia related in an uncharacteristically toned-down style, "behind this dizzy, wild thing who is your friend is a hurting lady. Okay? I can't tell you why, but for some reason, I never had much in the way of success with men. Loneliness, Jewel, it can make you desperate and these men, for whatever reason under god's universe, loved me."

"You never confided in me."

"Jewel, I was scared you would reject me."

"If you would have told me…"

"Desperation, it's a terrible state to be in. I don't care who it is, if they're in enough pain, they'll compromise principles they hold sacred."

"I guess it's no different from what I've been doing. Desperation. The word keeps coming up. It's what my life has felt like ever since…"

"It's a test, love. The more desperation we face, the more we'll sacrifice to stay alive. No matter how much it hurts, we're still going to try to survive it."

Jewel was being introduced to an unfamiliar, sober-minded aspect of her friend's personality; all while I was parking. I sat for a moment, romancing a gentle calm that unexpectedly appeared to triumph over a throbbing heart. I had just what I needed wrapped up in my gut; I was juiced up on courage.

When I reached the front door, I noticed it was ajar.

With minimal pressure, it swung wide open. Georgia noticed me standing at the threshold, but Jewel had her back to me. Even in my frenzy to get there, I convinced myself to stop at a shop and buy a single long-stem red rose. I held it in my hand. I eyed Jewel from behind for an instant while I witnessed Georgia's mouth widening.

"Oh boy, here comes a boatload of trouble," Georgia finally hollered, using her chin to communicate to Jewel that she needed to turn around.

When Jewel saw me, she made a dashing movement to get out of the room. I went into a sprint and was able to outpace her. I grabbed her firmly by the shoulders. For an instant, I was able to hold her in place while I tried to peer deep into her soul. But the grasp of my eyes on hers unnerved her and she struggled to loosen my grip.

"We need our life back," I forcefully decreed as Jewel continued twisting and pulling to break free from me. I held on. "Come on, Jewel. Please, just hear me."

"I heard you, Benny," she screeched. "You want the rest of the world to hear you too? I'm the chaff off the wheat…I was…"

"It's just not like that," I appealed with all my might.

"Oh, I see. I was so infinitely valuable you traded me in for a lollipop. "

"I never…"

"Oh, yeah. You did. You did!"

"This isn't the place…"

"Then why did you come here? I told you to get out; now get out!"

The timing was unimaginable. As Jewel was shouting me out, the door opened again. This time it was Garland; same old guy, joyful and self-assured.

"Was I invited to the party?" Garland smirked.

"He's your friend. You deal with him," Jewel yelled to me, her eyes daggers for both of us. She shifted her sight from Garland to me, back and forth several times.

"Benny, what's up?" Garland said, as if it were old times.

"I've come for my wife and family."

"You don't own us," Jewel protested defiantly.

"Now, I think you might be better off leaving her alone, Benny. She's happy with me; so are the children." He paused momentarily. "You made your choice."

"Happy?" Jewel countered. Breathless, she continued, "Let's not go that far. We haven't shared a genuine moment…"

"Jewel!" Garland moaned to argue the point.

"You speak, but your words never say a damn thing. You're so genteel, but you never feel; you're never real." Jewel confronted him with a look of disgust. Then, she stood to survey both of us with equal contempt. "Between the two of you, there's not half a man."

"Baby, you're just upset about Benny. Let's talk."

"Again, and again, and again. More of your lines," Jewel sneered.

"What lines?" we both uttered simultaneously.

Once again, Jewel had memorized just about every one of my songs. On this occasion, she had the mind to select the perfect fit. I had named the piece, "You Got Lines." From Jewel's perspective, she'd swallowed a pack of them. She was singing poison bullets, intended to send both Garland and me packing. Enraged at the scene, she blasted each of us by aiming lyrics, at times randomly yet some clearly with our names attached.

"Every time the situations arise, you got lines. You say you gotta hold me, when you see me, and keep us tight 'til the end of my life. He's breezy like feathers in the wind, says I'm his sensible wife.

"You need me, to keep growing, without me you would never survive. And this one, he's oh so confident and light, a little bit of laughter, and his touch of spice. You say I got, beauty and sass, I'm lively, caring, and so great to grasp. You want me, need me, must, could, gotta, should, but filled up with lust.

"Oh, I plea with you, stop this, I'm so confused. I've got a whole lot of love but I don't love it all, a couple of men that tear me apart." For the first time, she looked directly at me. "You want me to want you, but I can't it seems. I wish to hate you, but you shake me so deep, and then you smile, and suddenly, I'm weak at the knees."

It was the opening I'd never imagine getting. I unsheathed my "shining sword" to cleave in some lines of my own, "one, then the next, falling in rhyme."

"Oh I know it's not in my head when I turn to look you dead, in those eyes, you get shy, and you hold back a sigh. It's the little things I love, like when I'm giving you a hug and those hands slip deep in the back of my heart…"

"Stop!!" she shouted pitifully exhausted. "Well, well, well. Look what you seem to have packed tight and ready to go; lines, lines, lines…so sick of your lines."

Jewel left no doubt she was using her final statement to heap punishment on me especially.

"Jewel…" I entreated.

"What now!?"

"No lines, alright? Let me just tell you the truth. The evening all this mess began…"

"New York. Of course, I know. So what, Benny?"

"So, I lost faith that day. Then, the dying man telling me I had to do what was right…"

"You never believed that sort of nonsense," she screeched at the very top of her vocal range. "You interpreted it in a way that was convenient for you."

"I thought…"

"Well, you thought wrong."

"Jewel, I felt I was doomed and didn't want to take you and the children down with me. Can't you see that it all fell apart for me?"

I'm sorry…for all of us," she stated heartlessly.

"Me too. All I wanted was to take care of us better; I wanted to give you a finer life. I didn't know how," I wept.

"Benny, there's no road back," Jewel knifed at me. I could see a tear forming in each of the corners of her eyes as well. Her voice was quivering.

"Jewel, you don't understand."

"Damn it, leave me alone, Benny. I warned you I'd never tolerate unfaithfulness...now get the hell out of my life...go screw that two-bit whore of yours."

That was it for me. She looked at me with the worst sort of hatred I could imagine. She was breathing fire. Then her body turned away from me and she took a step; I could see she was about to bolt. My heart literally stopped beating—it was over and I knew it. It was the worst outcome I could have imagined yet one I knew had overwhelming odds in its favor.

I was about to tuck my tail between my legs and turn from her as well. What was the point of beating a dead horse? Faith wasn't offering me one last breath. Still, I knew there was one fact Jewel would never believe and I couldn't prove. It popped up to the tip of my tongue and had a mind to sneak out.

"What do you think happened between me and, well, you know?" I implored Jewel, unable to utter Cookie's name.

Jewels lips mocked me, her hands reached to strangle a neck she imagined in her grasp. Then a true miracle happened. I couldn't believe it; my eyes had to be playing magic with my senses, but the fact slid back down my throat and I swallowed hard. It had to be in less than a second all this occurred, but within that interlude of a fraction of time after I said the words, "between me and well, you know," well, the door...it opened again and... it was Cookie.

"Just what I need," I thought to myself. "Jewel's going to kill either me or Cookie, or both of us."

"Cookie, the two-bit whore, is that who you're referring to?" Cookie interrupted me.

"You!" Jewel yelled with outrage. "What are you doing here?"

"Figured the two of you could just maybe use my help...it's the least I can do," Cookie said contritely.

"And I've seen the most you can do," Jewel shouted her down.

"Cookie, remember that coupon?" I appealed.

"You bet I do. Jewel, IT...it never happened. Benny made up every excuse under the sun, but all the time I was with him he never touched me except to hold hands so he could put on a show to others."

"Don't you protect him! Don't you dare lie to me!"

"Benny never wanted me."

"Then, what in god's name were you two...?"

"I was just another piece of his genius plan. Jewel, he wanted you to think he was having an affair, so you'd hate him, kick him out, and find someone better," Cookie explained, pausing to be sure Jewel was hearing. "Would have been a perfect plan...but, too bad, you two love each other too much to make it work."

239

Jewel stood exhausted, her emotions thick as sap, too heavy to drip, as were the tears she was battling against.

Garland looked at Cookie, laughing gleefully. "Ditto that, darling."

"Ditto what?" Cookie asked.

"I'll admit I would have...but Jewel never let herself get cozy with me...hell, embarrassing as it might be, she not only never slept in the same room with me but I can't recall her even holding my hand," Garland whooped grandly. "You win, buddy. She's yours, Benny. Always has been yours...always will be yours."

Jewel looked at Garland, but with a bit less contempt than she'd expressed earlier. "Cookie may work better for you," she shot at him.

It was weird. Cookie and Garland glanced toward one other and gave a shrug as if to say it just might be. I hadn't the mind to debate it at the moment, but later thought that Cookie was really a deep person. Garland? She'd be too much of a handful for him. I doubted he'd ever be able to appreciate the value that a lady like Cookie possessed. Anyway, the whole situation was way over the top for Jewel.

"Oh, this is beautiful!" she cried as she ran out of the room.

We all stood speechless for some time. It was more than a little intense. I had not told anyone that I had never violated my bond of fidelity with Jewel. Of course, Cookie knew it as far as she and I were concerned. Why didn't I disclose it? Did I imagine that someday there might still be a future for Jewel and me? I can't answer that with certainty. I surmise that through the whole ordeal, I was dreadfully pained and had literally no sex drive, plus, infidelity, was unimaginable to me.

Had I ever considered that Garland and Jewel could have engaged in intimacy? I'll be shamefully honest and say I never thought about it. I was consumed with putting my plan into operation—I tried not to consciously address the gory details. I guess you could say I was lucky that Jewel had a firm standard dictating that she'd never have sexual relations with a man while she was still married to me. Then again, I'm sure that in my subconscious I knew it and that gave me a sense of security.

As for how Cookie knew to come to my rescue—that was the work of Craig. He figured out the secret I'd told nobody, including Simon, that I'd never attempted intimacy with Cookie (even he couldn't explain how he knew other than because of "instinct"). Based on his intuition, he called Cookie. After she confirmed his suspicion, he told her what was happening at my house. That's a miracle!

Well, now the main barrier to Jewel and me getting back together was removed. But that wasn't the end of it. She remained wrathful. Garland stopped coming by the Wright home, and I sacked out in the shit hole—I wasn't permitted in our home. At times, she wouldn't talk to me. It was touch-and-go much of the way; she had a lot of forgiving to do, and I wasn't convinced she was going to be able to do it. Still, I stayed the course, never letting up on her, following faithfully the "recipe" formulated by Cookie.

On a couple of occasions, I did talk with Garland. I wanted to hate him for everything he'd done, but I couldn't blame him for "doing what a man's got to do," especially a man like Garland.

One afternoon, he made a peace call to me. "I'll make it up to you. You'll see."

"Please, don't," I joked; but I was serious.

Other than being banished from my home, life was returning day-by-day to near normalcy. I was seeing the children almost daily, but the rule remained that I was not authorized to step foot in the house. Yet, as time went on, I sensed a softening in Jewel. I played it cool, keeping my presence in front of her at all times but not pushing too hard.

CHAPTER 18: THE HOMECOMING

During my exile, Simon had lovingly supported me. Patience was not my best virtue. Without his guidance, I might have caused the situation to stretch out much longer than necessary. Each time I met with him, he waved a yellow caution flag in front of me. Then one day, he again took out the green flag, his eyes glistening: I was to make my next move. Once more, the living space of my home would become the setting for a scene in the Wright family drama.

Shana was sitting alone at the dining room table reading a book. Jewel entered. Shana jumped up to greet her with a hug.

"Mommy, I want to have a woman-to-woman talk," Shana formally announced.

"A woman-to-woman talk? My, has my little girl grown up quickly."

"Well, I've been giving it a lot of thought…about you and Daddy. You have terribly mixed feelings now—about your husband—and that's understandable with everything that's happened. You've been hurt, and people have a tendency when they've been hurt to…"

Shana was interrupted as Dion entered, his headphones hanging lifelessly in his left hand. His neck was bent, allowing his head to hang in harmony with the headphones.

"My eyes are wide open now," he chattered to his mom and sister. "They're wide open, and I don't like what I see. I've been closing my eyes and dreaming of everything that'll never be real. But they're wide open now," Dion continued his passionless speech.

"What are you talking about, Dion?" Shana inquired.

"I stood on stage for the concert and everyone had their eyes locked on me, mic in one hand and the whole school in the other. The beat dropped. I poured my soul out. I hit every snare drum and tiptoed along every high hat."

"So what went wrong? What happened, Dion?" Jewel asked impatiently.

"After the show, I see my boy Manny being congratulated by everybody. People are using one hand to shake with him and another to pat him on the shoulder. But they didn't even say 'good job' to me. Not even a 'way to go, kid.' My eyes are open, and I see music for what it is—a dream."

"Music is a dream, Dion. It can even be a good one sometimes," his mom reminded her saddened son.

Interrupting her attempt to console Dion was a knock at the door. Shana ran to get it. It was Link. In his hand was a long-stem red rose with a card attached. He was dressed like the king's courier. Still ambulating with an uneven gait, he forced his body to stand proud and erect and deliver the special gift. It was a favor he said he would be honored to do when I asked him.

"Delivery!" Link called out. "Delivery for Mrs. Jewel Wright." He then reached for the card and opened it, trumpeting the written words. "One long-stem red rose for the person I love most."

"I wonder," Shana teased, "who might be sending roses?"

Link went on reading. "One long-stem red rose for my first evening coming home at two-thirty in the morning."

Link turned and walked off without closing the door. I had scripted the act. He progressed only a few steps before Craig passed him on his way to the door.

"Delivery!" Craig called out. "Delivery for Mrs. Jewel Wright." He then took the card attached to the rose and began reading. "One long-stem rose..."

"Mommy, what in the heck?" Shana laughed.

"One long-stem rose for your first step onto a sandy beach without me," Craig heralded.

Craig turned to leave and as he did, he passed Link on his way back again, holding yet another long-stem red rose.

"One long-stem red rose for every line I thoughtlessly put on you," Link recited the words on the card.

Craig returned, standing next to Link.

Craig read the one-liner on his card. "One long-stem red rose for every Sunday morning we didn't lay in bed together."

When he finished, I stepped in front of my friends, who then turned like soldiers and left.

I had purchased a new pair of black jeans and a black knit top that dropped off my shoulders like a grin. On my feet was a pair of shiny black leather boots. I'd combed my hair straight back with jell. Other than my wedding band, the only article of jewelry I wore was a small diamond stud in my left earlobe—I made sure I looked slick.

As expected, for the special occasion I'd prepared a new song—it was a beautiful piece, one I hoped would win her heart a second time.

"Is it too late to tell you dear, that every hour feels like a year, knowing you're in pain and I can't make it go and disappear. At first, I was alone, your hurt unclear and I could live in peace, thinking of your cheer. But now I only feel contrite, and I can't get through a night.

"Every second's like a day, every moment's bleak, an hour's like a year, a minute a week. A day is like a decade, a week's a score, a month's like a lifetime and a year is four. Every moment lives forever, every minute lasts 'til never, every hour's like a year, and every day is packed with tears.

"And I never knew the best thing for me was for me to be with you. So take me, take me, take me back, give me another crack and I'll stack up, take me back for the sake of tomorrow, take me back for my sorrow. It's g-u-a-r-a-n-t e-e-d to be a smile spree.

"Every moment lives forever, every minute lasts 'til never. Every hour's like a year, and every day is packed with tears."

When I finished, I embraced Jewel. Then the children joined us and we all stood together for a few moments. We were holding hands and all of our eyes were closed as we tilted our heads to the sky above.

"Lovin' ain't an easy thing, Jewel. You said it best. But I'd move heaven and earth one long-stem rose at a time and work my whole life at it with you."

"Benny…" Jewel spoke with a full release of emotion. "The pain you put me through, you've put us through. It's been unbearable. But I look in your eyes and somehow I can't help but love you at the same time I hate you. For the sake of us, for the sake of our family, you earned yourself a shot."

Both of us were flush with emotion and dropped into each other's arms.

"I've had better plans," I admitted. "If it's okay with you, I'd like to come home now."

Jewel nodded, giving me the Indy 500 final-lap winning flag.

"This is still going to take some time to heal," Shana warned. "Feelings may get jumbled up for a while," she advised as she turned to address her mom. "You may be experiencing love one second and disdain the next, but keep remembering this moment…and you'll get through it." Then, she moved her eyes to take in her father's attention. "That goes for you too, Daddy."

"Thank you, Dr. Wright," I said, noticing at the same time that Dion was looking somber. "And what's wrong with you? Things are looking up now, man."

"Not really," Dion responded curtly.

"School concert," Jewel explained. "Didn't go too well it seems."

"Welcome to the Highs and Lows Club, son," I said to Dion as I draped my arm over his shoulder. "The road is long and winding…but who wants their roads short and straight anyway?"

"Mom," Shana interrupted with a thought that she didn't want to forget. "You said we could go to the Angel Face concert Friday."

"Daughter, call and get tickets."

"How many?" Shana ranted excitedly. "Can I call now?"

"Sure," Jewel responded. "And get four; we'll all go."

"I'm not going," Dion harshly protested. "I'm done with music."

"Quitter, quitter, pumpkin…quitter," Shana teased.

"Pumpkin quitter, Shana?"

"Yeah," she answered tentatively to her brother, sensing she'd made a blunder.

"I can't take it. Sorry, Dad, but I'm not screwing my life up TOO, waiting for a miracle," Dion said as he jetted out of the room.

"Get those tickets," Jewel ordered to Shana, "and make it four."

"He won't go; you know how he is," Shana sighed.

"Over my dead body he won't." Jewel then turned to address me. "Kid's got a size ten hurt and a size eight heart. That's the difference between men and women," she philosophized. "Women know they're short on heart and long on hurt and surrender. Men think they can win and will fight to the death trying."

"That must be why I'm still fighting, love."

"And with your son following you stride for stride," Jewel smiled.

Shana had already swirled her body several times as she ran to the phone and pressed numbers to order the tickets. She was on hold.

"Your call may be monitored for quality purposes."

Shana repeated the message she was listening to on the phone, taking her index finger and directing it at her temple as a gesture of absurd futility. Then, she continued to speak the words she heard on the line. "Thank you for your patience. All operators are currently busy helping other customers. Your call is very important to us and will be handled by our next available agent in the order received. If you'd like to order online we can assist you at www.blahtickets.com. Your wait is currently two minutes." Shana addressed her mom. "Mom, do they say that to everyone?"

"Only to you, Shana."

"I hope there's still good seats." Shana then spoke inaudible words into the phone. A second later she addressed me. "Daddy, there's a man on the phone for you. I had to put the ticket people on hold."

"Let me take it," I insisted.

"Daddy, don't forget the tickets," Shana noted as she ran into the kitchen.

"I'll handle it," I assured her as I began talking into the phone. "I couldn't do that…I'm sorry. Well, I'll tell you what…okay, I have an idea. Sure, I can help you out and you can help me," I nodded resolutely. "It's going to work perfectly. Thanks. Bye."

After the call, I lingered by the phone and then hung up. Shana saw me as I started to walk toward the kitchen.

"What happened to my call?" she asked worriedly.

"Oh, my, I…"

"Daddy, you forgot?"

"I'm kidding."

"You got them?"

"Quick as a wink," I smiled.

"That fast?" Shana questioned the improbability. "You got them that fast? Did you get amazing seats?"

"Good enough, my girl. Now, let's eat dinner."

I returned to the dining room table. Jewel measured me carefully, perceiving a subtle glimpse of a devious smile. Shana shrugged and proceeded to help her mom.

"Daddy, you're not quitting on your music," Shana asked as she snuck a look at her brother, "like some people I know."

"No. I learned my lesson about giving up on things you love. In fact, I just finished some new tracks." I addressed Dion. "They're about me; they're for me. I don't care if the rest of the world hears them, Dion. They're for the people I love. It's about our story"

"That's good because you're not going to make a lot of money printing home CD's and having your friends at Jimbo's listen," Dion belittled.

"I still believe you'll make it, Daddy. I feel it…right here." Shana pointed to her heart.

"You just keep that hope alive…and know I'll be here for you, Shana."

"I can't wait to see MY MAN, Angel, again." Shana let her words waft, like a swooning love sound.

"Oh, speaking of Friday night, that call I just received

was about a meeting after work. I can't miss it. Big opportunity. Big, Jewel. Your man may be up for a huge
raise. I might have to meet you at the concert."

Jewel eyed me a second time with bemusement. Her
sense of trust might take months or years to be fully
restored.

CHAPTER 19: WRAPPING UP

What should have been the last scene of this tale, our family once again cemented as one, was not. Things changed after the call I received while Shana was waiting to get tickets for the Angel Face concert. Everything fell into place; now the setting for the finale would take place at the Friday evening concert that I would attend with my family.

Angel Face was playing one night only at the Fox Theater Detroit—even for the up-and-coming artist it was an honor to play in this esteemed venue.

The consensus amongst those living in our city might easily be that the Fox is the finest Detroit has to offer in indoor forums. The theater is magnificent by every measure and standard. Its old elegance has served for decades as a stage for the most famous artists in the world, from Mariah Carey to Sting to Moody Blues to Janet Jackson to Led Zeppelin to Keith Richards.

The ceiling canopies the audience in dazzling yellows and oranges with a touch of blue. The ambience is regal yet classy at the same time. No wonder Angel Face admitted how excited he was to play for the first time to his hometown fans in the best the city has to offer.

The concert was totally sold out. Shana, Dion, and Jewel had taken their seats. The one empty place next to Jewel was awaiting my arrival. To the side of Shana, sat Craig. Behind them were Link, Garland, Jimbo, and Cookie. Off to the side was Simon, though none of the group knew who he was. The facility wasn't too far from my work, and they were expecting me at any moment.

"I can't get over these seats, Mom," Shana crowed.

She had every right to be thrilled. They were sitting about nine rows back and slightly off from the center, in the orchestra section.

"These must have cost Daddy a brick," Shana concluded.

"It's a mystery to me how he did this. I wonder if Garland owed Daddy a favor," Jewel voiced loud enough to make sure Garland heard.

She intentionally turned toward him, but Garland never gave a clue.

"Garland doesn't do favors," Dion said dubiously. "We'll get it out of Dad when he gets here."

"However we were blessed to get these choice seats,

there's only one way better to do a concert," Craig commented.

"Yeah, be on stage," Dion concluded with his normal glumness.

The lights flickered several times. I still hadn't arrived. Shana was fidgeting in her seat.

"So much for promises. I don't know what to do about that man," the little adult stated with wonderment. "He's going to miss the opening."

"If you'll all take your seats, please…the show will be beginning soon," the announcer informed the audience.

Anticipating the start of the concert, everyone already seated commenced to join in rhythmic clapping. The noise rose as the excitement increased.

"Your attention, please. Sadly, due to illness, Flip Side, who was scheduled to open for Angel Face, could not be with us tonight." He paused, but not long enough to let the disappointment expire. "But wait, please. We're excited to announce a special opening act. The man has been around forever, but he's agreed to come out for what he insists will be the crown jewel of his career. You're going to love it! Trust me when I tell you to put your hands together and give a big welcome to a man who just finished writing a musical called…*Wrapped*. That's right, it's…MAAAGIC!!"

The crowd was caught off-guard. Still, the unexpected performer was greeted with a loud round of applause—Jewel, Shana, and Dion appeared as if they each had just taken a punch in the belly; they were the only three in the audience who sat motionless, not clapping… or breathing.

I was standing to the side of the stage. The lights brightened, and I could be seen raising my right arm high above my head, pointing my index finger as if in communion with my God—I ran to center stage and grabbed my mic. I stood for a moment. My head was raised high and my eyes were closed.

"Welcome to the show! I couldn't be more thrilled to be here," I rejoiced. "This is very special for me…it'll be the last public performance. My career may not have been what I dreamed," I paused to reflect on my words, "but my dreams are fulfilled. In front of me, are the three people that I love most in the world.

"I'll admit that I took a few wrong turns to get here, read a couple signs incorrectly. It ended up being a long, grueling journey; but I fought for what I believed and fell in love with the fight to do what I thought best for the people I love.

"I had lots of obstacles to overcome, many I put in my own way. Yet, I even fell in love with those brick walls placed in my path, because I fell in love with breaking them down. At times, I sat in front of them, mourning and moping, letting them feel like a cold stone wall. But finally I fell in love with standing up to those insurmountable barriers. I learned the hard way that I just needed to put on a smile cheek to cheek and get to hammerin' through whatever was holding me back.

"I wrote this music as a reminder to me…and for any of my friends out there stuck in the grind…to play whenever you're busting through hard times and tearing down concrete walls. I wrote it because I want to be right there with you, because it's my favorite thing to do."

The music seemed to stream from a million speakers, from every seat, ceiling panel, and molecule of matter. I knocked out the final song of my creation, *Wrapped*. I titled the song, "Window to the Sky."

"I've got my window open to the sky, ain't no cloudy day gonna break my high. My window's open to the sky, and I'm waitin' with a smile for the sun to shine. I had a view that could blow my mind, and opened the world to my shielded shrine. On the evenings in July, I saw bluebirds on moonlit vines. Red clouds cloaked the trees, on a dawn in the middle of an autumn breeze. Roses bloomed from leaves, with a grace that could carry me to peace with ease.

"But then times got tough, and the days got dark and the dark got stuck. Months passed by, mired in dusk and I lost my desire and lust. So I stained my window with a painted glaze, 'cause I'd given up on sunny days. But the moment I did, I was livin' in a hopeless pit. I was dead inside, no hopes at all, nothing to pray for, nothing resolved. I just longed to see haze and fog, at least I could hope to see something evolve.

"I've got my window open to the sky, ain't no cloudy day gonna break my high. My window's open to the sky, and I'm waitin' with a smile for the sun to shine. Nobody likes it when the months spill rain, everybody's wished that their window was stained. But once you give up and throw it away, you'll never see the sun again, no way. You'll never see the light and that's a-okay, if you never had a taste of a summer day. But when you get it and you see the view, you can't live life in a hidden room. You'll just cry, and you'll dream of sky, dream of clouds and dream of light. You'll even dream of rain on gloomy nights, and dream of lightning strikes.

"Somehow, someway I got my windows back today, and this time, come rain or shine, I ain't paintin' no window of mine.

"I've got my window open to the sky, ain't no cloudy day gonna break my high. My window's open to the sky, and I'm waitin' with a smile cause the sun's gonna shine."

The music transitioned, ending with a reprise of "Get Moved," the song Garland performed for me that first night after my return home from the tragic trip to New York.

While the audience was getting moved, I gazed out at Jewel, our eyes locked; it was the same bond we'd had from the beginning of our love—stretched, frayed, and battered, but as durable as it had ever been.

The audience couldn't get enough of *Magic*. They

implored me to come back for four encores, delaying Angel Face by fifteen minutes—I'm blushing.

Finally, I jumped down to the seat level and took Jewel in my arms. I peered at her and whispered my love before kissing her for the first time ever during a performance.

I had resolved that it was the last time I'd play second, or third fiddle at a show; that it was the last time I'd ever take the stage as a performing musical artist.

EPILOGUE

"No man can survive without a god."

I found it odd that after all my discussions with Simon he'd surprise me with that statement. I'd have predicted him to be an agnostic.

When I had completed the songs for the piece I called *Wrapped,* I asked him if he'd like to hear it. He responded that he'd hesitated to ask me before I made the offer but had thought many times that he would like to listen. About a week later, he called me and asked if we might meet so he could return the disc and the accompanying notes I had outlined for him. When I did see him, he complimented me on the music and then made a surprising request.

"If I'm out of line, please don't be bashful about letting me know. You can think about it, but I was wondering if

I could be honored to help you write the story. I'm not a bad writer and I'm an even better editor."

"It would be my honor to have you onboard," I proudly answered.

Then he proceeded with a second query.

"I respect that as a career you're retired from music. But I was wondering if you'd let me take *Wrapped, The Musical,* after it's completed, and show it to a friend who owns a tiny theatre here in town. He might get a kick out of it. Hell, he might even want to put it on."

"Of course, you can," I responded.

"Well, before you agree to have me partner with you, I have an idea. What if I do the Epilogue? Like a sample of my work to see if you're comfortable."

"Begin at the end? Sounds off, but what else could I expect from you?" I needled him.

"Come on. At least that way, I can't screw up the beginning," Simon winked.

"I might be best off to let you hijack the whole project."

"Nope. You'll have to do the telling but I can be your coach."

A long period would transpire before Simon would deliver to me his version of the ending of *Wrapped.* By then our relationship had graduated to a full friendship. He'd met my family and likewise I'd met Patty, his fiancée. Even more astonishing, just before he presented me with what he had prepared for the Epilogue, instead of offering me jelly beans he came prepared with the three flavors of See's suckers.

I'd never had one but he insisted they were the best in the world, suggesting I try the caramel or chocolate. I selected the latter, and after pulling off the thin covering, put it in my mouth. He was right—we were delayed the time it takes to imbibe the great flavor before I could read. The candy quickly converted me to a See's addict.

The words of his written sample touched me. I'll present them exactly as he scribed them for me.

> *No human can survive without a god.*
>
> *The catch is that we only call on Him or Her at those moments in our life when an event causing overwhelming uncertainty has served as syringe and needle to inject into the veins of our soul the sensation of fear. That's when we stand alone, terror-stricken and humbly confused. Without God we'd perish, for those experiences can be deadly to the physical and psychological mechanisms of our species.*
>
> *In that sense, God is all we have ever conceived. His force can grace peace on enemies, turn violent killers into repentant wimps, bring rain where drought promises starvation, and cure a dying sinner of disease. All this and an endless number of other miracles, God can perform to demonstrate his mercy, forgiveness, and love.*

If it sounds like The Man is a sucker for coming to the rescue only when one of His subjects has their chin in the dirt, think again. Those events of biblical proportion, that He is so famous for, are delivered at His discretion. We can call out for mercy all we wish, but we will get an answer only if He is so inclined, and the motives that might drive Him to satisfy a plea are as fickle as a child's love of parent, for what Mommy or Daddy does or does not do for them.

Needless to say, it's a tough relationship between the individual human being and their God. Man tosses Him out like an enemy when life is peaceful and secure, or when He fails to gratify a wish, but always begs for His return when the going gets tough—it's a love-hate relationship, immutable and infinite, yet at the same time, from the human's perspective, fragile and conditional.

What's for certain is that it's a one-of-a-kind relationship every individual has between themselves and their superior power. It's also a dynamic association that can redefine itself at any instant and in any of an unlimited number of ways.

Benny had been to hell and back. He'd been a buddy of Satan and a foe of God. He'd been alone without realizing he had a friend left in

263

the world. He'd cried to be forgiven, to take back the wrong he believed he'd committed.

When it was all over, what happened? Jewel embraced his wounded soul. She healed the pain he brought home after wandering virtuously for months. It was Jewel who loved him back to health. It was Jewel who always loved him. It was Jewel who forgave not his sins but his sacrifice.

Benny will call on God again in his life. He's no different than the rest of mankind. But his hopes and dreams will have the best chance of being satisfied through human love.

Benny and I spent hours talking together. One afternoon he made a disclosure to me, setting off a remembered conversation between us.

"It came to me during the time I was writing 'Every Moment Lasts Forever, while I was waiting for my wife to grant me the right to share our marital bed again with her,' Benny explained." I realized I was finished pursuing music as a career.

"I had my time, Simon. I had my opportunities…they just never broke for me," he shrugged. "Getting that call to perform at The Fox Theater absolutely confirmed it. It was a tease."

"A tease?" I queried him.

"I believe that sometimes we're tested. A temptation is placed in our path to weigh our resolve to do what we know is true for us."

"It's still sad that you turned down the chance to achieve what you had been working toward all those years."

"No, it's not really. It was an opportunity I needed a decade before, but when it finally came to me it wasn't right. Timing, it just wasn't there. So when I received the call while Shana was waiting to get tickets for the Angel Face concert, my first reaction was to say no. Then it dawned on me that it would be the perfect situation for me to formally retire. That's why I agreed to do the opening act at the concert."

"Felt good?"

"It was great fun actually. I'd never performed for that large an audience, so it was the perfect forum for saying goodbye. No way was I going to compete with the guys in their late teens or early twenties that were coming out. And I'll tell you something else. The most difficult thing along the way was facing myself, accepting that I really didn't want it. Had I attained what I was reaching for, it likely would have destroyed everything that was precious to me. It nearly did.

"I didn't cop out, Simon, if that's what you're thinking. I'm a smart man. I've already had a great promotion at work and recently an offer for a position at another company making twice what I do now. My job is to support my family; that's my responsibility. I'd say I've matured a lot as a person from all of this...I've grown up."

I honestly didn't know whether to laugh or cry. I was truly happy for Benny and respected what he was doing. Yet, I couldn't put to rest the part of me that had been aroused to root for him becoming a star. It was sad knowing that this man I now considered a true friend had sentenced his dream to be executed, and that he had willfully carried out the punishment.

As he sat next to me, I could see that Benny was genuinely at peace. That's what elevated my spirit and helped me whip the sorrow with a sweet philosophic take on the whole situation—sometimes our dreams, fulfilled or otherwise, serve no purpose other than to promote us evolving to become complete and loving humans.

Benny Wright was true to the heart of Benny Wright, and it didn't matter if that was judged right or wrong by anyone else. The man was content to live out his existence in Detroit,

stroll along the path of his life with his hand
clutching his wife's, watch his children tackle
the same challenges he'd confronted, and try to
be there to support them through it.

"Simon," I said after finishing his draft of the Epilogue, "you're hired."

"Let's get rolling."

We did.

Simon followed through not only on his pledge to coach me writing the story but he also delivered *Wrapped* to his theater friend.

"My un-esteemed friend at the un-esteemed Saber Theatre in the un-esteemed Highland Park area of the un-esteemed city of Detroit fell in love with it," he informed me.

Then, after complimenting the piece, he said the theater director had a brainstorm: all the characters in the story could play their real roles on stage since every one of them lived in Detroit. Simon presented the idea to me.

"What would it be? 'The Adventures of Ozzie and Harriet'?" I smirked, referring to the 50's TV series my grandma had told me about, where a real family comprised of a mom, dad, and two sons put on a weekly show about the events that occurred in their daily lives.

"Why not? It's perfect," Simon encouraged. "Who could act the parts better? Every one of you is talented.

Maybe it'll take the scowl you keep telling me about off teenage Dion's face," he poked at me.

"I'll think about it and talk with Jewel and the children, okay? I'll get back to you within a week," I promised him.

It was six months almost to the day after that conversation that *Wrapped* opened. My family, along with the other characters, put on the show. We all agreed it was a blast.

I might conclude by mentioning that I had never made public the true story behind *Wrapped*. However, the owner of the theater concluded it would be a nice promo for the opening to have a taped interview of me. He contracted with a tiny production company in Detroit. I was immediately offended by the attitude of the host, Mr. Conrad, and refused to complete the remainder of the interview if he was kept on.

"Simon," I excitedly greeted him on the phone. "I talked to your friend at the theater, Martin, and told him we needed someone else to do the taping. Guess what we decided? Guess who's going to do it?"

"No idea...okay, Jay Leno?" he quipped.

"Better," I said enthusiastically. "You!"

"What if I object to you crying?"

"No problem. I'll have you wimp out for me."

THE END

OTHER NOVELS COMPLETED AND UPCOMING BY

Dennis A Nehamen

Mistaken Enemy
Insatiable Hate
Mescalero Blood
Crushing Steel
Musicball
DOGMAi
The Making of A Madman
Misty's Place
The Greatest American Outlaw
Music and Murder
Juliette

ABOUT THE AUTHOR

Dennis A Nehamen, Ph.D. is a forensic and clinical psychologist who has authored novels, screenplays and musicals, including the award-winning musical *Wrapped*. He lives in Los Angeles with his wife and has two adult children.

www.ingramcontent.com/pod-product-compliance
Lightning Source LLC
Chambersburg PA
CBHW070813180626
46818CB00001B/247